SWORD ART ONLINE

PROGRESSIVE

007

REKI KAWAHARA
ILLUSTRATION BY abec

"I-I'm not entranced by anything!"

Kirito

A swordsman striving to reach the top floor of Aincrad. He's a solo player by nature but has decided to team up with Asuna for now.

"What's up, Kii-boy? Entranced by Big Sis's beautiful legs?"

Asuna
A girl trapped inside the game of *SAO*. She used to be self-destructive but now works hard to help beat the game.

Argo
The mysterious info dealer of Aincrad who comes and goes as she pleases. Known as Argo the Rat.

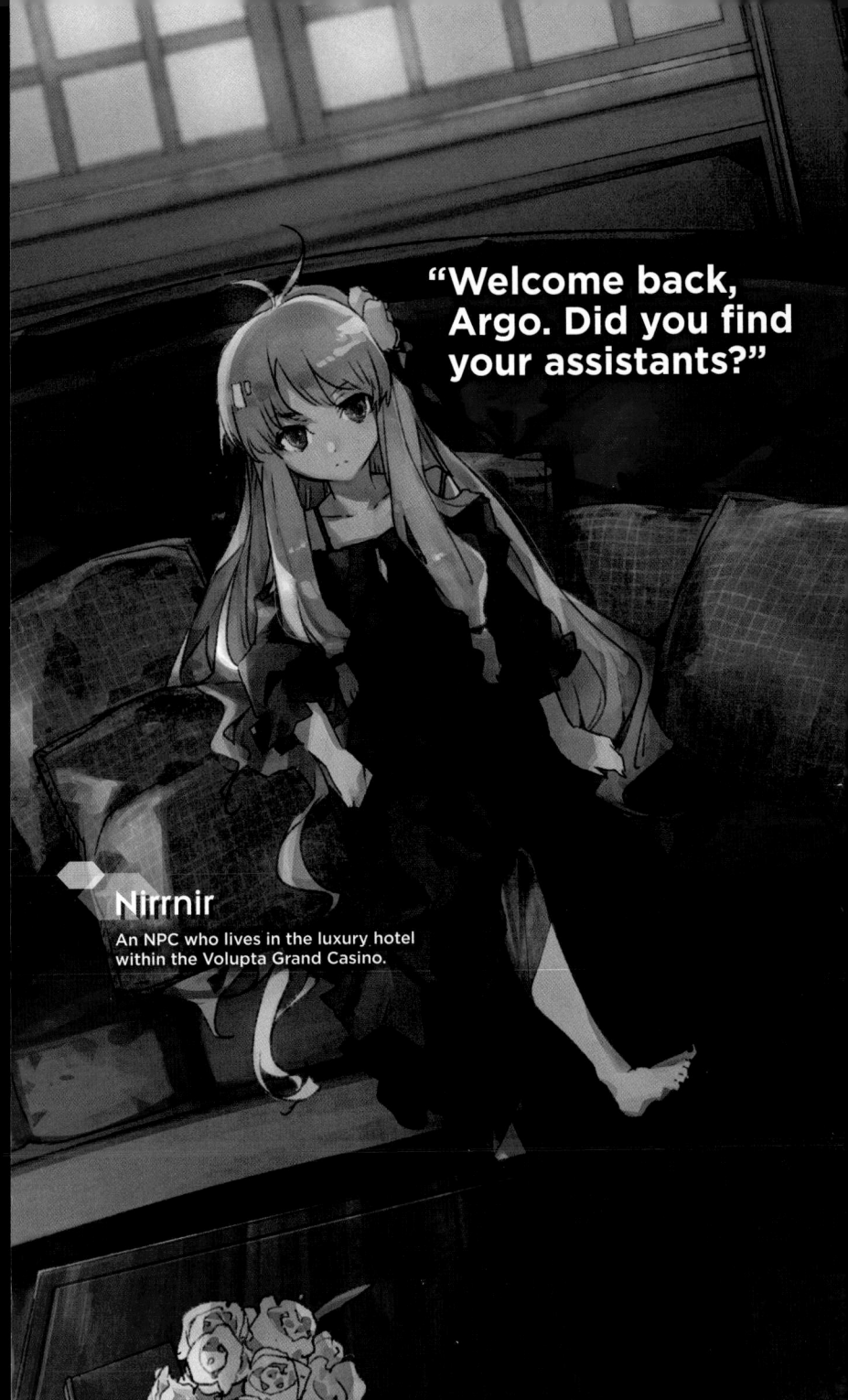

"Welcome back, Argo. Did you find your assistants?"

Nirrnir

An NPC who lives in the luxury hotel within the Volupta Grand Casino.

Kio

An NPC who serves Nirrnir.
A battle maid armed with an
estoc and a breastplate.

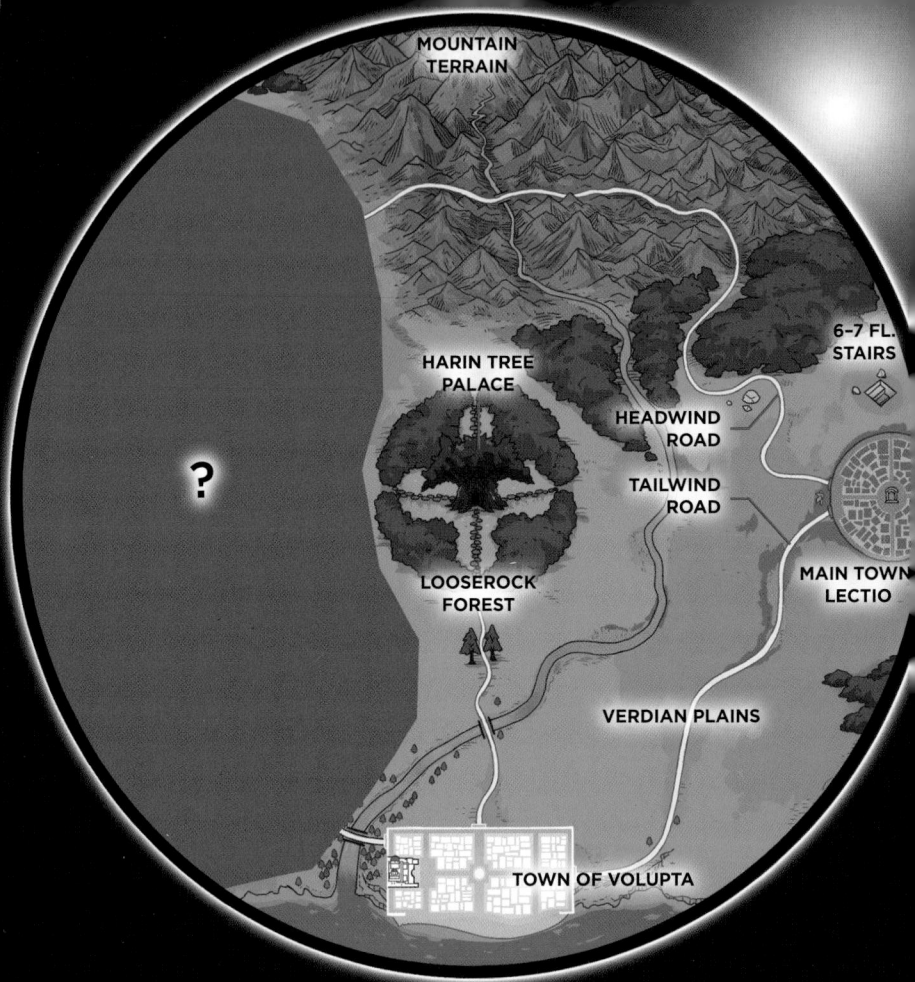

Map labels: MOUNTAIN TERRAIN · HARIN TREE PALACE · HEADWIND ROAD · TAILWIND ROAD · 6–7 FL. STAIRS · LOOSEROCK FOREST · MAIN TOWN LECTIO · VERDIAN PLAINS · TOWN OF VOLUPTA · ?

FLOATING CASTLE AINCRAD FLOOR DATA   AINCRAD

SEVENTH FLOOR

The seventh floor has two main features. The first is its eternal summer climate. Kirito and the other player arrive in January, right in the middle of winter in the real world. But the blazing sun and humidity of midsumm blanket the entire floor.

The other feature is the casino. The starting point of the seventh floor, the town of Lectio, is on the easte end, while the labyrinth tower is on the western end. There are two roads leading there. One is Headwi Road, where treacherous terrain and numerous monsters await. The other is Tailwind Road, where the path gentle and few threats exist. Traveling down Tailwind Road leads to Volupta, a town with a very large casi

Volupta's casino offers all sorts of gambling, including plenty of card games, dice, and roulette wheels. T biggest draw of them all, however, is the Battle Arena—a monster coliseum.

All the monsters there are from the seventh floor, and battles are one-on-one. There are five battles duri the day and five at night. Many players went broke here during the beta test.

Map Illustration: Tatsuya Kuru

SWORD ART ONLINE PROGRESSIVE

VOLUME 7

Reki Kawahara

abec

bee-pee

YEN ON

New York

SWORD ART ONLINE PROGRESSIVE Volume 7
REKI KAWAHARA

Translation by Stephen Paul
Cover art by abec

SWORD ART ONLINE PROGRESSIVE Volume 7
© Reki Kawahara 2021
Edited by Dengeki Bunko
First published in Japan in 2021 by KADOKAWA CORPORATION, Tokyo.
English translation rights arranged with KADOKAWA CORPORATION, Tokyo, through Tuttle-Mori Agency, Inc., Tokyo.

English translation © 2022 by Yen Press, LLC

Yen On
150 West 30th Street, 19th Floor
New York, NY 10001

Visit us at yenpress.com
facebook.com/yenpress
twitter.com/yenpress
yenpress.tumblr.com
instagram.com/yenpress

First Yen On Edition: January 2022

Yen On is an imprint of Yen Press, LLC.
The Yen On name and logo are trademarks of Yen Press, LLC.

Library of Congress Cataloging-in-Publication Data

Names: Kawahara, Reki, author. | Paul, Stephen (Translator), translator.
Title: Sword art online progressive / Reki Kawahara; translation by Stephen Paul.
Description: First Yen On edition. | New York, NY : Yen On, 2016–
Identifiers: LCCN 2016029472 | ISBN 9780316259361 (v. 1 : pbk) |
    ISBN 9780316342179 (v. 2 : pbk) | ISBN 9780316348836 (v. 3 : pbk) |
    ISBN 9780316545426 (v. 4 : pbk) | ISBN 9781975328146 (v. 5 : pbk) |
    ISBN 9781975383336 (v. 6 : pbk) | ISBN 9781975339913 (v. 7 : pbk)
Subjects: | CYAC: Virtual reality—Fiction. | Science fiction.
Classification: LCC PZ7.K1755 Swr 2016 | DDC [Fic]—dc23
LC record available at https://lccn.loc.gov/2016029472

ISBNs: 978-1-9753-3991-3 (paperback)
        978-1-9753-3992-0 (ebook)

10 9 8 7 6 5 4 3 2 1

LSC-C

Printed in the United States of America

"THIS MIGHT BE A GAME, BUT IT'S NOT SOMETHING YOU PLAY."

—Akihiko Kayaba, *Sword Art Online* programmer

SWORD ART ONLINE PROGRESSIVE

RHAPSODY OF CRIMSON HEAT (PART ONE)

SEVENTH FLOOR OF AINCRAD, JANUARY 2023

1

"IT'S HOT!"

That was the first thought that escaped the lips of my current combat partner upon teleporting to the seventh floor.

"*So hot?!*" she repeated for emphasis, scowling upward. For structural reasons, we couldn't see the blue sky or the sun itself, but the light that radiated down from the bottom of the floor above us was undeniably stronger here than on the sixth floor.

"It's supposed to be midwinter here...so why is it so hot? In fact, when we stopped by for a bit last night, wasn't it a lot cooler than this?" she asked, turning back to me.

I shrugged. "I feel like I mentioned somewhere along the way that it depends on the specific floor whether they model the real-world season or not...This one probably just ignores the season entirely. It was cool last night, but it wasn't *cold*, right?"

"I know, but it's January 5. It feels like it's eighty-one degrees here," she said, an oddly specific number to quote. Elsewhere around the teleport square, there was only a handful of other players, but all the same, she hurried over to the shade of the broadleaf trees at the edge, then opened her player menu.

After a quick manipulation of her equipment mannequin, she removed her red hooded cape. Underneath it were a thin breast-plate and a leather skirt that stopped just above the knees.

With a shake of her lustrous chestnut-brown hair and an

equally long sigh, my partner, the level-21 fencer Asuna, looked me over with a grimace.

"Kirito, why don't you take off that coat? It's making me sweat just looking at it."

"Uh, I dunno…" I said, looking down at my avatar. "Your hooded cape is more or less a cosmetic item, but my coat is my primary source of armor…If I take this off, I'll lose most of my defense."

"Not in the safety of town, you won't."

"True…"

Logically, she was correct, but the memory of being attacked by an NPC assassin in the midst of the sixth-floor town was still fresh in my mind. I at least wanted to stay fully equipped outdoors, but it was true that the interior of my black-leather coat was rising on the sweat index.

The town attack was part of a forced event, so I shouldn't have to worry about it happening again, I told myself, and I went into my menu to return the Coat of Midnight to my inventory. Underneath, I wore a breastplate similar to Asuna's, a thin shirt, and long pants. That would be much cooler to wear—I thought.

"Doesn't really change much…" murmured the fencer, staring me up and down. "I think it's the all-black thing. It just *looks* hot. Don't you ever feel like wearing a different color, Mr. Black?"

"W-well…you've been wearing red ever since I first met you," I argued back.

Asuna glanced at the red tunic she was wearing and looked up with a smirk. "I wear other colors here and there."

"Uh…you do…?"

"When I'm relaxing at the inn, yes. But when we're outside, I have no choice. I have to wear what gives me the best defense."

"Y-yeah, well, that's what I was saying!" I argued, but the truth was, defensive numbers weren't the only reason I wore nothing but black. My main coat was the Last Hit bonus prize for beating the first-floor boss, so the color wasn't my choice, but the shirt and pants were regular store-bought clothes, and I could choose a different look if I felt like it.

Technically, I could claim another practical reason—that dark-colored gear offered a bonus to Hiding—but that could also backfire, depending on the terrain and brightness. I'd chosen dark blue when I created my character, and I didn't consider myself to have always been enamored with black or anything like that. Maybe there was some connection to the fact that my middle school uniform was the stuffy, traditional *gakuran*, a long-sleeved, high-collared jacket, that made me feel comfortable in dark colors...

I was pondering this very belated topic when Asuna snuck up and patted me on the back. "Well, I'd feel weird if you started wearing white or orange, so I guess I'll put up with you looking sweaty. Anyway, let's get moving."

"Moving...Where?"

"It's our first time in this town, right? Well, second...But obviously, I'm talking about lunch. Do you have any recs?"

"Ah...Let's see..."

I blinked and turned to survey the square.

Lectio, the main town of the seventh floor, had a very orthodox design by the standards of Aincrad. At the edges of the teleport square were homes and shops built from stone, wood, and plaster in the half-timbered style.

In contrast to the board-game-like town of the sixth floor, Stachion, the roads leading outward from the circular plaza here were complex and confusing, and I spent several days based out of this town during the beta test. I tried out a number of restaurants in that time, of course, but my memory of them was oddly faint.

"Lectio, Lectio...The best dish of Lectio was..."

I tried to summon my memories, but they were proving stubborn. It was as though someone had clamped a lid down on my mind...

"Ah..."

I gasped, at last realizing why my memories of this place were hazy.

I was the one who put that lid on them. It was a place where I'd experienced great sadness.

Recalling those tragic memories was the icebreaker that made them all come flooding back in miserable detail...

But for now, I let them run off into a side tributary and focused on Asuna's question.

"Sadly, there wasn't really anything in the beta that I'd call a great specialty here. For one thing, Lectio isn't the main encampment of the seventh floor."

"Huh? But it's the main town, isn't it?"

"On paper, yes. Anyway, I can explain that part later. Let's get to a restaurant first. Umm...I think that one over there sells pita-ish sandwiches, the one in that direction has chicken-ish rice, and the one that way serves some spicy-ish stew."

"...What's with all the -ish foods?" Asuna asked suspiciously. Then she followed it up with, "When you say chicken and rice, is that Japanese style or Singaporean style?"

"Huh...? What's the difference...?"

"Japanese-style chicken and rice is kind of like an *omurice*. It's basically fried rice with chicken, flavored with ketchup. Singapore-style chicken and rice is thin-sliced poached chicken over ginger-flavored rice. It's called Hainan chicken, or *khao man gai*," she explained smoothly. I just stared at her.

When I met her on the first floor, she said stuff like "I didn't come to this town to eat good food," but now that we'd been working together all the way up to the seventh floor, I could say with certainty that Asuna's knowledge of food outclassed the average *SAO* player's by far. I would have thought that meant she liked to cook food as much as she enjoyed eating it, but the five skills Asuna currently owned were Rapiers, Light Metal Armor, Tailoring, Sprinting, and most likely, Two-Handed Lances. It was too early to have two crafting skills at this point, but why did she pick Tailoring instead of Cooking? And why was she working on Two-Handed Lances, a skill with hardly any use for her...?

We'd been partners for over a month at this point, but there were still so many things I didn't know about her, I realized.

"It was probably more on the Singaporean side. I don't remember if the rice was ginger flavored, though."

"Why are you so fuzzy on this one...? Regardless, let's go to that one."

"You like Hainan *gai*?"

"You're mixing them up. It's Hainan chicken *or khao man gai*!" she snipped. Then she added, "It's not me, it's my br...my family that likes it. I just felt like having it, since it's been a while."

"...Oh."

I grinned to hide my surprise. It was extremely rare for Asuna to speak about her real family. The last time I could remember her doing so was in Yofel Castle on the fourth floor, when she'd told me that her Christmases on the other side were spent eating cake all alone, waiting for her father and mother to come back home.

Be that as it may, I had no problem with having chicken and rice for our first meal on the seventh floor.

"Let's go, then. Right this way, madam," I offered, bowing obsequiously and pointing an upturned hand in the right direction. Asuna sniffed smugly and took the lead.

We headed down a path southwest from the teleport square and, following vague memories, turned right once and left once. A pleasant smell hung in the area. Asuna's nose started twitching, and she smiled.

"Yes, this does have the smell of some proper chicken and rice."

"Just don't expect the exact thing," I replied, although my hunger gauge was nearly at its maximum, too.

The Irrational Cube, boss of the sixth floor, went down around eleven o'clock last night. Asuna and I went up the staircase from the boss chamber to the seventh floor and activated the teleporter in the main town there, then returned to Stachion to escort the NPCs Theano and Myia home after their help in the fight. We stayed at an inn in Stachion because we were utterly exhausted, and I slept a dead, dreamless sleep until nine in the morning.

The bulk of the frontline players would have been busy working on the seventh floor by then, so we spent an hour relaxing around the place before checking out, then teleported back to Lectio through the gate. So looking backward, the last time I ate anything was before entering the sixth-floor labyrinth tower. And that had only been an informal meal of a doner sandwich from a cart. I couldn't even remember the last time we sat down and took our time eating at a table.

Clearly she was thinking the same thing, because Asuna's pace picked up as we rounded the last corner and came to the restaurant on the right side.

It was a very simple business with a round wooden sign hanging over the open doors. The relief carving on the sign said in English: MIN'S EATERY.

"Min's Eatery...? What's an eatery?" I asked, unfamiliar with the word.

Asuna explained, "It's like a casual restaurant or a café. This place looks small...I hope there's an open table."

Her prayers were answered—there was no one in the place. It was a bit too early for lunch, and the way to get here was convoluted and out of the way, so if I had to guess, I'd say hardly any players knew this even existed yet.

The smaller-scale *eatery* term was accurate: There were six spots at the counter and a pair of tables for two, nothing more. We sat down at one of the tables, and before we could even look at a menu, a voice from behind the counter bellowed, "Welcome! What'll it be?"

"H-hey, give us a second!" I protested to the plump woman there, whom I took to be Min herself. I opened the wooden menu on the table so we could look at it. As a general rule, the menus and signs for NPC shops in Aincrad were written in English. At first, I found it difficult to read and decipher them, but over time you started to figure it out—or at least get used to the concept—and so lately I felt like just glancing over the letters was enough to tell me what they were. Maybe.

Fortunately, the folding menu had only two starters, two main dishes, and four drinks. At a glance, the starters looked like salad and soup, and both of the main dishes were rice-based. One was chicken, as I remembered, and the other one looked like basil rice. Both dishes were forty col for a large portion and thirty for the regular size. That was a reasonable price for the seventh floor, considering it was meant to be a light meal. However…

"…Basil rice? Is that the same basil that comes on pizzas and stuff?"

"…I would assume so. It's spelled the same," agreed Asuna.

Under my breath, I complained, "But…basil's just a leaf! They're going to charge the same price for leaves and rice as they do for chicken and rice? That's crazy!"

"I don't know why you're complaining to me………Ah!" She blinked with surprise, then smiled. "I get it! I don't think this is just leaves on rice. It must be *kaphrao*."

"Ka…*kaphrao*? Have I heard of that before…?" I wondered.

She patiently explained, "I was just telling you that the name of Singaporean chicken and rice is *khao man gai*, right? That comes from Thai. And the two biggest rice dishes in Thailand are *khao man gai* and *kaphrao*."

"Ohhh…and what *is kaphrao*?"

"It's often just called *kaphrao* rice in Japan. You stir-fry chicken or pork with basil, then serve it with rice."

"Ohhhh…I don't think this place served that during the beta, though."

"Maybe the owner went to study in Thailand before the game launched," she said with a very serious expression; I couldn't tell if she was joking. Asuna then sighed and said, "I can't keep waiting. If you don't decide what to order in the next five seconds, I'm making the decision."

"Ah! W-wait a sec!" I cried, staring at the two items on the menu. *Do I go with the safe choice of chicken and rice? Or live on the wild side and try the unknown* kaphrao *rice?* I let myself waver for four seconds, until inspiration struck.

"…Wanna order both and share them?"

"That's a good idea," agreed Asuna. Then she added quietly, "Make them both larges."

That time spent studying in Thailand must have served her well, because Min's chicken rice and *kaphrao* rice left nothing to be desired. Maybe the "secret sauce" of coming in absolutely famished helped, but I was certain that the chicken was nothing at all like the beta test dish of simple boiled chicken on rice. The *kaphrao* rice was a new taste for me, spicy and delicious.

Asuna and I finished off our shared dishes in less than three minutes, washed it down with vanilla-scented tea, and sighed with great satisfaction.

"…Hey."

"Hmm?"

"You said this town wasn't really famous for any food. I'd say this was quite the find, wouldn't you?" Asuna asked, arching her eyebrow.

I replied with what I'd been thinking about as I ate: "It wasn't this good in the beta. It was like…dry, lonely rice with underwhelming pieces of chicken…"

"But it was definitely rice, right? Isn't this the first place in Aincrad we've seen that sells a proper rice dish?"

"Oh…"

She might have been right about that. I'd eaten some porridge gruel in the dark elf camp on the third floor, but that was closer to barley boiled in sweet milk, with nuts and dried fruits sprinkled on top. I wouldn't have called that a rice dish, by any means.

"I think you're right," I said. "But the rice here is long-grain rice, isn't it? That's good, too, but it doesn't give you that good ricey feeling after a full meal that short-grain rice does."

"…How do you know about long-grain and short-grain rice but have never heard of *khao man gai* and *kaphrao*?" Asuna asked in disbelief.

"Uhhh…because I went on a field trip in elementary school to try out planting rice in a paddy…?"

"Ohhh, that's nice. We didn't get to do that…Although I did go catching bugs in a paddy once," Asuna said with a smile. She quickly composed herself and cleared her throat, feeling like she'd been talking too much about the real world.

"At any rate," she continued, "this was really delicious. Thank you for showing me to this wonderful place."

"Y-you're welcome. Doesn't feel like we're celebrating a New Year's meal, though."

"First of all, it's already January 5, and it's sweltering outside. They could serve a traditional New Year's dish here, and it still wouldn't feel right," she said with a shrug, finishing her iced tea and looking out the window. The interior had good ventilation, so it was fairly cool, but the sunlight flooding through the noon-time window was as full and suffocating as a midsummer's day.

Because the beta test had occurred in August, every floor felt warm and summery, but none had been so bad that it felt uncomfortable. Maybe the heat of the seventh floor had been amped up, just like the flavor of the chicken and rice here. If so, given how unpleasant it already was for Asuna and me in our light armor, it was going to be hell for the tank players decked out in full-metal plate armor. The same could be said for the dark elves, who didn't seem to enjoy the heat.

Asuna was thinking the same thing. "I hope Kizmel's all right," she murmured.

"Hmm…Well, it might be hot here, but there's plenty of greenery and water. I don't think she'll have as much trouble as in the dusty desert of the sixth floor," I explained.

The fencer looked surprised by my comment. "No, I'm not talking about the heat. I mean about the keys."

"…Oh, r-right."

That should have been the primary concern.

Asuna and I were in the midst of the "Elf War" questline, on the side of the dark elves. We helped Kizmel, knight of Lyusula, with a sequence that saw us recovering one of the sacred keys on each floor. We'd found the Jade Key on the third floor, the Lapis Key on the fourth, the Amber Key on the fifth, and the Agate Key on the sixth, with two remaining. But an unforeseen event had caused all four sacred keys to fall into the hands of Kysarah, the adjutant of the enemy Fallen Elves.

The big problem was that it was unlikely to have been a pre-programmed part of the quest story.

There was a gang of player-killers out there in Aincrad, led by a mysterious man in a black poncho. At some point, they'd joined up with the Fallen and helped them steal the keys. All six keys were recoverable in the beta test, but we'd just lost them all partway through. This couldn't have been part of the original questline story, because it happened through the interference of another player.

We parted ways with Kizmel just after it happened on the sixth floor. Kysarah broke her favorite saber, but I'd offered her an Elven Stout Sword as a replacement—it was my backup weapon— so I wanted to believe that our connection wasn't permanently severed. But Kizmel had to report to the dark elf high priest or some other important figure to explain how she lost their sacred keys. There was a price to be paid for her failure.

Hoping to cheer Asuna up, I did my very best to enunciate loudly and clearly. "Remember what Kizmel said when we left her? *I am one of the queen's own royal Pagoda Knights. Only Her Majesty and the knight commander have the right to formally rebook me.* I'm sure she'll be fine. Once we get started on the next chapter of the quest on this floor, we'll see her soon after."

"...Rebuke."

"What?"

"It's rebuke, not rebook. It means to punish someone for their failure," Asuna explained, her worry replaced by annoyance. She exhaled and looked me in the eyes. "Yes, you're right. If I have enough time to sit around moping, it would be better spent doing something. Now that we're full again, shall we get started on the seventh floor?"

My temporary partner extended her fist across the table. I smirked.

"You bet. First things first, though—we gotta upgrade our equipment."

I pounded her knuckles, and we got to our feet.

2

AS OF JANUARY 5, 2023, THIS WAS WHAT ASUNA AND I had in terms of skills and equipment:

Kirito, level-22 swordsman, skill slots: 5
    Skills in use: One-Handed Swords, Martial Arts, Search, Hiding, Meditation
    Equipment: Sword of Eventide +3
        Coat of Midnight +6
        Fortified Breastplate +4
        Skintight Shirt +2
        Trousers of Shadowthread +5
        Spiked Short Boots +3
        Ring of Brawn
        Sigil of Lyusula

Asuna, level-21 fencer, skill slots: 5* (6)
    Skills in use: rapiers, Light Metal Armor, Tailoring, Sprinting, two-handed lances
        * (Meditation)
    Equipment: Chivalric Rapier +7
        Woven Hooded Cape +2
        Thinly Made Breastplate +6
        Fencer's Tunic +4

Pleated Leather Skirt +4

Prancing Boots +3

Earrings of Ripples

Ring of Luminescence

Sigil of Lyusula

* Skill in parentheses is from Crystal Bottle of Kales'Oh.

The recommended challenge level, accounting for the safety margin, was typically the floor number plus seven, so neither Asuna nor I had any reason to hold back on tackling the seventh floor, statistically speaking. Half our gear was rare quest rewards or boss drops, but that was far from all of it. In my case, the breastplate, shirt, and boots were ordinary store-bought items, and so were Asuna's cape, tunic, and skirt. They were powered up, but their absolute numbers were still far short of the rare loot, so the first thing to do when we reached a new floor was to check out the NPC shops and see if we could buy anything that was an improvement on those items (preferably at a bargain price).

It was a crucial part of survival in this deadly game, but it was also part of the fun of playing an RPG.

But after observing the shelves of the first armor shop we went into, Asuna muttered "This selection isn't exactly inspiring...and it's the biggest shop in the main town" just quietly enough so the shopkeeper couldn't hear.

I nodded. "Yeah...Unlike the eatery, this place hasn't been upgraded, it seems."

"I take that to mean it wasn't impressive in the beta, either?"

"My memory is hazy, but that is the impression I recall."

"You had such vivid and detailed memories of Stachion. Why is your knowledge of Lectio so vague?" she asked, pointing out my failing again. I pursed my lips.

In order to explain why, I'd have to touch upon the tragedy that befell me—that befell nearly every beta tester—on this floor. I would have preferred to keep that memory locked deep in my mind, never to be spoken of again, but Asuna was too sharp. I wouldn't be able to hide it from her.

I cleared my throat and said, "In order to explain why, we will need to get to the town's exit."

"…That's fine. There's nothing much to buy here anyway."

"Let's go, then."

I led a skeptical Asuna back to the teleport square. There were still few players to be seen, either because of the heat or because there wasn't much to see and do here.

I wanted to take off both my coat and breastplate, but I told myself the heat was only virtual, and I concentrated on crossing the square, taking the east-west main street through the town to the west to do so. It wasn't a very big town, so just a few minutes of walking brought into view the wall that separated the safe zone of town from the dangers of the wilderness.

"…Huh?" Asuna murmured to my right. "Why are there two gates?"

As she said, at the end of the main street were two large gates with a nearly identical design. The only difference between them was the marble sculpture atop each one.

The sculpture on the right was a miserable-looking man, his back hunched over a cane, as though walking against the elements in a storm.

The sculpture on the left was of a decadently dressed man, his back arched, holding an enormous wine glass.

Each gate was open, offering a clear view of the terrain on the other side. Beyond each gate was a path surrounded by green grassland. There was nothing in between the paths on the far side of the wall, so there was nothing stopping you from going out one gate and taking the other path instead. So the meaning of the two gates was…

"…To put it dramatically, I suppose they reflect the fates that await players beyond the gates."

"Fates…?" Asuna repeated, clearly thinking this was overly

dramatic. She glanced at the gates again. "Then…the path out of the right gate offers hardship, and the path out of the left gate is the easy road, this would suggest."

"That's mostly right," I replied as we reached the open space just before the gates. There were no players here, either. Most likely, the two big guilds, the Dragon Knights Brigade (DKB) and Aincrad Liberation Squad (ALS), had already chosen a gate and headed onward.

Once we were there, the perspective effect on our visibility changed, making it possible to see clearly out into the wilderness. In the distance through the right gate, under the statue of the man with the cane, was a thick forest and a craggy, bald mountain. On the left gate side, under the man with the wine, the path seemed to sit on flat plains as far as the eye could see.

"So um…Lectio's on the eastern edge of the seventh floor, right? Meaning the labyrinth tower is on the western edge?" Asuna asked.

"Yes," I confirmed.

"And where's the starting point for the 'Elf War' quest here?"

"Should be in the center of the floor. It's roughly equidistant from whichever path we take."

"…So we should probably take the easy path then, right?"

"I suppose so. But only if you have an ironclad will, Asuna."

"All right, what's going on with you and these cryptic statements? What do the two paths have to do with your memory of this floor?" she snapped. I could tell that her irritation gauge was rising, so I resigned myself to the difficult conversation ahead.

"Well, uh…The right path has lots of monsters and treacherous terrain, which is tough, but that's the normal game-type route. The path on the left has few monsters and flat land…but there's a huge town along the way. It's about two or three times bigger than Lectio."

"A huge town…? Is it a dungeon?"

"No, it's a human town. Safe zone, inns, shops, the whole deal. Good food, too."

"So what's the problem?"

"The problem is…there's a huge casino in that town."

"Huh…?" Asuna's mouth hung open. She looked up at the sculpture of the man with the wine glass, then back down at me again. "A casino, like…a casino-casino? Like in Las Vegas or Macau?"

"Like in Las Vegas or Macau. Not that I've been to either," I said, gazing through the left gate. Like it or not, the bitter memories of the past were flooding back into my mind. "Out of the thousand players in the beta test, I'd estimate that over eighty percent of them took the left path. And the majority of them got hooked on the casino, and the majority of *them* got taken for all they had. Rumors said that half the beta testers dropped off after playing on the seventh floor."

"……"

Asuna was silent for a good five seconds, then walked around to face me directly, blocking my view.

"And what happened to *you*?"

"……I lost everything," I said, grimacing bitterly. "All the col I'd saved up from adventuring, all my rare items, everything. I only had my sword left…but I didn't give up. I got back on my feet again from there and headed for the next floor. I might have lost at the casino, but I didn't lose at the game. No, I didn't lose at the ga—"

"Right."

"Wh-what?"

"We're going right," Asuna declared, cutting off my heroic saga, and she began to walk toward the gate under the man with the cane.

I didn't argue with her choice; it wasn't like I wanted to make the same mistake twice. Particularly because, in the beta test, dying just meant coming back to life on the first floor, but there would be no starting over in your underwear this time. If I lost all my money and equipment, I'd have to wait around in the Town of Beginnings for someone else to beat the game for us.

But...

Something inside me—perhaps my gamer's soul—refused to let me stay a loser. I faced Asuna's back and said something she didn't expect to hear.

"The beach."

"...Huh?" She turned around.

I told her gravely, "Didn't I mention this before? On the south side of the seventh floor, there's a beach with white sand and palm trees. That's part of the casino town in question...Volupta. Of course, it's not a real sea, just a bit of a lake that reaches the edge of the floor. But the water itself is salty."

"A beach......"

She repeated the word, very conflicted. She glanced up at the bottom of the floor above, which was radiating sunlight and heat, then looked at me again.

"But...with this heat...the beach should be packed with people, right?"

"Actually, in order to earn the pass with beach access, you have to win a ton of chips at the casino. And I doubt the DKB or ALS are going to get sidetracked with gambling," I said, thinking of the stern expressions of Lind, leader of the DKB, and Kibaou, leader of the ALS. Asuna took a step closer to me, wearing a very similar expression.

"But that means *we* can't visit the beach without betting at the casino, either."

"W-well, yeah...But when I was telling you about that, do you remember what you said, Asuna? That if the seventh floor is eternally summer, you were going to do *something* at the beach..."

"......"

Asuna just blinked, taken aback. Then her eyes darted away in a very awkward, unnatural way, and she grunted, "Ummm."

"Ummm?"

"Uuuuhhh..."

"Uhhhh?"

She jabbed me in the side. So apparently she wasn't speaking in some nonhuman tongue, after all.

"...How much does that pass cost, if you converted it to col?"

"Uhhh...If it's the same price as in the beta, one casino chip is worth a hundred col, so it'd be...thirty thousand col?"

"Thirty K!" she shouted. I couldn't blame her. My current net worth was about ninety thousand col, and I guessed Asuna's was around the same. It would be insane to spend nearly a third of that for a chance to play on the beach. And yet...

"N-no, not so fast. The beach pass isn't bought with three hundred chips. You get it from the casino once you've won three hundred chips' worth of games. So it's kind of like, uh, a VIP benefit..."

"...Meaning that once we've got the pass, we could cash in all our chips back to col?"

"Unfortunately, you can't convert chips into col, but you *can* trade them for items with a high resale value, so you can sell them and make back the money," I said, silently adding in my mind, *Assuming you can actually win three hundred chips!*

"Hmmm..."

Asuna folded her arms and considered this information. After all this, if she decided she still wanted to go right, I was prepared to go along without a fuss.

Ten seconds later, the fencer unfolded her arms, looked up at the sculpture of the man with the cane, then examined the man with the wine glass.

"...Even if I won thirty thousand chips, I still wouldn't lord it over anyone like he's doing."

"...Uh-huh."

"Well, let's go," my partner said, briskly walking toward the left gate. I followed her without a word.

Of the two paths that extended from the Gates of Choice in Lectio, the NPC residents called the right (northern) path the Headwind Road. The left (southern) path was the Tailwind Road.

Of course, that wasn't a literal reference to the direction of the wind but a figurative one. The left path that we chose was pristinely paved with bricks, with flowery fields on either side. The road was ever so slightly tilted downward the entire way, and we saw virtually no monsters.

"…If only it were a little bit cooler, this might be the most pleasant trip I've had yet in this place," Asuna commented.

I stifled a yawn and agreed. "The meadows on the second floor were nice, but only if you ignore the occasional runaway bull…"

"Ah yes, the cow floor. I'd enjoy a chance to eat that enormous shortcake again."

"The Tremble Shortcake? Hmm, maybe I should have teleported back to Urbus, eaten the shortcake and gotten the luck bonus, and *then* tried the casino," I commented ruefully.

"That buff only lasts for fifteen minutes," she pointed out. "You'd never make it in time."

"You never know! If I sprinted for all I was worth, I might have enough time to play one game with it active."

"You really just wanted to gamble, didn't you…?" Asuna said, right as a deep buzzing of wings sounded nearby. We drew our swords and took a stance with our backs to each other.

Monsters hardly ever appeared on Tailwind Road, but that didn't mean the few that did were pushovers. Their stats were par for the seventh floor, and their attacks were complex, so you had to be on your guard.

Asuna scanned the northern side of the road, while I looked on the south side. When the wings picked up again, I heard her cry, "Get down!"

I ducked as far as I could, resisting the natural urge to turn and sneak a peek. Something passed just over my back at a ferocious speed. I looked up and saw a green shape hovering in the air about thirty feet away.

It was an insect about twenty inches long, with translucent wings. The silhouette was squat and round, but there was a long, sharp horn extending nearly the entire length of its body from its head. The pale-red cursor displayed the name Verdian Lancer Beetle.

"...What's Verdia?" Asuna whispered.

"The name of these plains, I think?" I murmured back. "Uh-oh, it's coming again!"

The hovering insect lifted its sparkling emerald carapace. *Vmmm!* It buzzed the air and darted directly toward us.

The horn of the lancer beetle, which first appeared on this floor, was powerful enough to punch a hole through plate armor at full speed. It was nearly impossible to parry with a one-handed weapon; the only way to guard against it was with a sword skill, but even then, it wasn't easy to hit that sharp horn when it came blazing at you so quickly. If you failed, it would go through your chest or head, and a critical hit counter could prove instantly fatal.

Asuna and I crouched to avoid the lancer beetle's charge. I got to my feet immediately, turning around and staring at the insect as it took a gentle turn over the field.

"Well, we can avoid it...but this seems endless to me," Asuna murmured.

I shrugged. "It's not endless. As you avoid its charges, their angle gets lower and lower. So eventually, we won't be able to duck under it anymore."

"Then what should we do?" she asked. As a beta tester, it would be easy for me to simply give her the answer, but by this point, I wanted her to develop the observational skills and instincts to put together a strategy against an unfamiliar monster type. I wasn't necessarily going to be there to help her forever.

"Can you tell what its weak point is?"

"...Underneath its body?" Asuna replied at once.

Should've known, I thought, impressed. "Technically, it's the ganglion right in the middle of the place where all six of its legs meet. The brain's a weak point, too, but they're usually heavily armored, and that giant horn makes it hard to aim at it."

"But how do we attack its undersi—" Asuna started to say, but

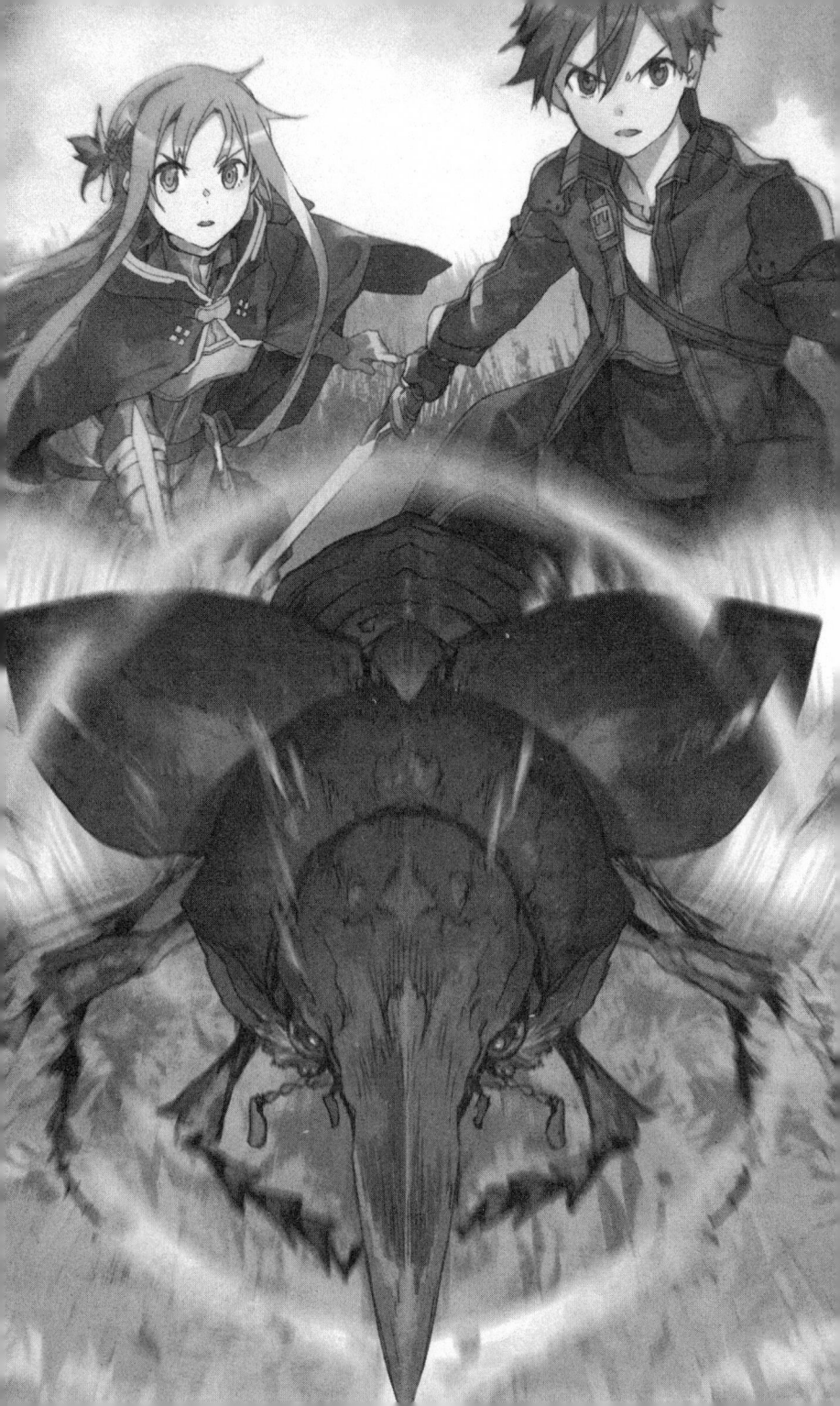

the lancer beetle lifted its wing sheaths as high as they could go, the sign that it was about to charge again.

When a lancer beetle charged, only its head, prothorax, and wing sheaths were visible. Each part was covered in tough armor that was highly likely to deflect any normal attack. If you attempted a sword skill and failed, it could deliver a fatal counterattack.

But by way of a hint, I started the motion for the single-hit skill Vertical. Next to me, the tip of Asuna's Chivalric Rapier wavered with indecision.

But then it went perfectly still, and she assumed the stance for the charging skill Linear. Our swords took on a high-pitched whine and faint glow.

Right on cue, the lancer beetle started its third charge. I resisted the urge to duck, waiting for the right moment. Asuna kept perfectly still, holding her active sword skill in wait. With just the barest of hints, she'd figured out the tactic that took me two deaths in the beta to figure out.

The deep buzzing of its wings immediately growled louder, a sound that summoned a kind of primal fear. The wickedly sharp point of the horn was just ten feet away when the two of us fell to the ground—but on our backs this time.

The lancer beetle's less-armored belly passed right over our faces. A normal swing would do almost no damage while we were lying on our backs, but a sword skill was different. As long as you maintained the right distance and angle between body and sword, the skill would activate, even if you were on the ground. Unfortunately, you couldn't get that extra boost of power from pushing off the ground, but that wasn't necessary to hit the belly of an insect-type monster.

""Haaah!"" we exhaled in unison, unleashing Vertical and Linear.

Blue and silver light flashed, and two swords struck true at the base of the lancer beetle's legs, cutting it deeply.

They made a terrific *wham!* sound, the sign of a successful critical hit. The monster's squat body shot upward, spraying crimson damage effects, and went into a tailspin. It took three or four of these attacks to defeat one in the beta, but my level and sword were considerably more powerful—and doubled by the presence of my partner. Based on the physical sensation of the hit, I guessed that one more hit would do the job. I pushed off the ground with my free hand and got to my feet.

"That was it! Now let's do that agai..."

But the spinning lancer beetle fell to the ground, bounced, then went still in the middle of the air, unnaturally. It briefly contracted, then burst into blue particles. Countless shards flew out, then melted into the air, gone forever.

"...Huh?" I gaped.

Asuna almost sounded disappointed. "Oh, it just takes one hit?"

"Well...technically, that was *two* hits. But even then...I wonder if they nerfed its hit points..."

Or maybe it's some new death-mimicking skill, I thought, but there was a window that displayed the col, experience, and items we'd earned. Asuna sheathed her rapier and began examining her rewards.

"Oh, this floor is interesting. They're giving us a ton of money and experience. But the items are...all crafting mats."

"Hey, don't look down on insect parts. They can make armor that's way better than what you find in stores...as long as you don't mind the look..." I admitted, scrolling through my own items to the bottom of the window.

Then, forgetting that we were out in the dangers of the wilderness, I howled, "*Ooooohhh?!*"

"Wh-wh-wh...*what*?!" Asuna shrieked, startled. I hit the ITEM MATERIALIZE button, then grabbed the object that appeared over the window and turned around to face her.

"Ta-daa!!"

I thrust an eight-sided prism crystal under her nose. It was colored a deep-rose pink, similar to garnet.

Sadly, my temporary partner did not seem to understand the

value of the item. She just looked at it, then me, then back to the crystal again.

"…And what is that?"

"Umm…it's called a healing crystal."

"Oh, is that the thing you were talking about?" she said, her face lighting up at last. She snatched it out of my fingers and held it up in the sunlight. "Ah, so this is what they look like…and this really heals all your HP, all at once?"

"Yep, sure does."

"How do you use it?"

"Well, obviously, you chew on the end…" I said, then realized that it probably wasn't a good idea to joke about how to use the crucial item that would be our lifeline in conquering this game of death. I cleared my throat and took the crystal back from Asuna. "Okay, I'll be serious. Using them is very simple, and it's the same way for all crystal items. First, you tap the surface of the crystal, then select USE from the menu that appears. Second, you hold it in one hand, then touch the other end either to yourself or the person you want to use it on, and then you say '*Hea…*' Yikes!!"

I hurled the healing crystal. Asuna caught it, shouting, "H-hey! Why did you just throw it at me?!"

"Er…You're supposed to hold it, and just say '*Heal.*' But I very nearly used it on you when you already have full HP," I explained, feeling a cold sweat break out on my forehead.

Asuna sighed deeply. "Didn't you use these things all the time in the beta? You should know better."

"Not all the time. Even on the tenth floor, they were a rare and valuable item…And let me tell you, I wasn't the only tester who was saving them and ended up dying because we didn't want to waste them."

"Well, you'd better not do that now. If you or your partner is in danger, don't hold back, just hea—Yikes!!" she shouted, without warning, and tossed the healing crystal as though it were red-hot. I caught it.

"……"

"……"

We stared at each other without a word. Eventually, Asuna murmured, "You should probably put that away now."

"G-good idea," I agreed, opening the belt pouch on my left side, but I stopped there. "No…You should have it, Asuna."

"What? It was your loot, so it's yours, Kirito."

"In our partnership, I'm the vanguard, and you're the rearguard, right? It's just good tactics to have the crystals in the possession of the back row, because they have a better vantage point of the battle," I said intently. I held out the crystal, but Asuna only pursed her lips.

I wasn't just making that up. Players on the front line had to focus so hard on the enemy up close that they could lose track of their hit points, and usually you were using both hands, so to utilize a crystal in the midst of battle, you had to let go of your weapon or shield.

On that point, I already had my left hand free, so I *could* hold it in my hand to use it, but to my good fortune, Asuna didn't point out the hole in my logic; she accepted the crystal.

"…I don't appreciate being labeled the back row, but I take your point. In that case, I'll hold on to this."

"You're not just holding on to it. Like you yourself said, you'll need to use it without hesitation when you're in danger."

"……Mm." She nodded, dropping the crystal into her belt pouch.

A sudden thought flickered through my mind: *Maybe I should have kept it.* That way, I could avoid using it on myself as long as necessary, holding onto it for Asuna's benefit as much as possible. Wouldn't Asuna agree?

In that case, both of us should keep the crystals. Healing and purification crystals were very rare in the beta, but we just got one from the first monsters we fought on the seventh floor. Perhaps they revised the drop rates to make them easier to find.

Asuna looked around the field, seemingly having the same train of thought.

"…Hey, are those stag beetles the only ones that drop healing crystals?"

"Not at all. Some monsters drop them more often, but from the sixth floor on, every monster has a tiny chance of dropping one."

"Tiny chance? Like…how tiny?"

"Umm…Well, this is only according to what was researched during the beta, but they found that the chance was 0.01 percent on the sixth floor, and 0.1 percent on the seventh floor…I think."

"0.01 percent…? Meaning you might get one for every ten thousand monsters you beat?!" Asuna exclaimed, arching her eyebrows.

I shook my head. "That was for the sixth floor! We beat tons and tons of monsters on the sixth floor and never got a single crystal, right? But on the seventh floor, it's a tenth of one percent, so…"

"That's still one in a thousand!"

"Y-yeah, I know…but they might have improved the odds since the beta," I said hopefully. Only then did the puffs of rage over Asuna's head calm down.

"…Well, we *did* get the drop from the first monster. So… since there's no one else around, want to try hunting more stag beetles?"

"Sure…"

I glanced at the clock readout in the corner of my view. It was one fifteen in the afternoon. Even at a casual pace, it wouldn't take us two hours to get to the gambling city of Volupta, so we could kill an hour or so hunting before we continued on, and it still wouldn't be dark yet.

"…Then let's do a little monster farming and practice beating lancer beetles."

"Roger that!" said Asuna with a grin. She stepped off the path into the field to the north.

Over an hour and a half, Asuna and I beat about fifteen Verdian Lancer Beetles; about ten Verdian Poison Wasps, a powered-up version of the wasps from the second floor; and about five Greasy

Worm Lizards, creatures that oozed up out of the earth like a cross between a snake, an earthworm, and a lizard.

One monster every three minutes was a significant pace on the Tailwind Road, where monsters were few and far between. Asuna quickly mastered the tactic of using sword skills as you fell, the trick to beating the lancer beetles. Aside from the one time she fell to the ground using the new tactic, only to freak out when she saw a Greasy Worm Lizard wriggling up from the dirt right beside her, our hunting went very smoothly.

We got plenty of money, experience points, and materials, but unfortunately, not a single extra crystal. Thirty monsters, of course, was not nearly a large enough sample size to gauge whether they'd adjusted the rates, but at the very least, it didn't seem like they'd be dropping all over the place.

"...What should we do? Keep trying a bit longer?" asked Asuna, holding her rapier.

I considered the question and then replied, "No, we should wrap it up now. If we keep trying, we're not going to be able to reach Volupta before it gets dark."

"Is that a particularly bad thing?" she asked.

For a moment, I wasn't sure what to say. I couldn't come right out and tell her it was because Volupta was an enchanting sight in the sunset. Instead, I looked up and offered weakly, "Well, it's our first time down this road, so we might get lost in the dark, you know..."

It wasn't even three o'clock yet, but the light around us was already starting to turn rich and golden, and you could tell the temperature had dropped a fair bit.

"How could we get lost? It's a single path...But fine," Asuna agreed, sheathing her sword. I placed my own in the container on my back and walked us toward the brick road.

"It's funny...We've been hunting for an hour and a half, and not a single other player has come this way...I wonder why?" I asked.

Asuna looked down the road both ways, seemingly realizing it for the first time herself. "I suppose you're right…Do you think the DKB and ALS and Agil's group all chose the Headwind Road?"

"Huh? The only benefit of that route is that you eliminate the risk of going bankrupt."

"…That just makes it sound like *we're* at risk of going bankrupt."

I hunched my shoulders, ruing the mistake of saying anything at all, and pointed to the southwest. "W-well, let's just get going. Once we get to Volupta, you'll see that there's plenty to do aside from the casino."

Despite her skeptical expression, Asuna said nothing more on the matter, and we hurried down the brick road as the hints of nightfall crept closer.

3

WE ENCOUNTERED ALMOST NO MONSTERS FROM that point until we were done crossing the three-mile Verdian Plains.

The moment we crested the final hill, Asuna exclaimed "Ohhh!" and ran a few steps forward.

Before our eyes was one of the—if not *the*—most elegant and beautiful cities we'd seen in Aincrad thus far. It was like something out of a fantasy world—well, it *was* in a fantasy world, but even still.

The city sloped gently downward to the left, with all the pure-white stucco houses arranged on descending levels. The larger dwellings had roofs painted a pristine deep blue, and they shone in the golden light of the sunset like bonfires. It was stunningly beautiful. In the beta, it was made of gray stone like the main town, so the entire place had been renovated for the official release. Beyond the bottom row of houses was a white-sand beach with emerald-green water.

This was what I wanted to show her, and it worked. Asuna stood still in amazement, then exhaled and murmured, "It's beautiful...Just like Santorini..."

"Santorini...? Is that a real place?"

She looked at me, rudely awakened from her momentary

dream. "Yes, it's a real place. It's a Greek island in the Aegean Sea. There's a town there called Oia that's identical to this one."

"Uh-huh…" I was tempted to ask if she'd actually been there herself but decided against it. Instead, I asked, "Then maybe they modeled it after that one. Is Oia famous for having casinos?"

"Hmm…I've heard that there are casino resorts in Greece, but I don't think there are any on Santorini."

Again, I decided against asking her how she knew that. Instead, I shrugged amicably. "Interesting. Well…Look there, on the far side of town."

I was pointing to an especially large building, looming all the way on the other end of the layered town. On either side of an octagonal building with a cobalt-blue roof were towers with conical tops. It looked like a palace. That was the Volupta Grand Casino, the place that inflicted joy and despair on so many players in the beta test.

"…That's the place?" Asuna asked.

I nodded. "Yes. Listen to me, Asuna—that casino's going to test our willpower in every way possible. Don't get too heated, but don't be too timid. Stay calm but be bold…"

"Yeah, yeah. I get it," she said, clamping her hand over my mouth to stop me from talking. "Let's go earn three hundred chips, enjoy some time at the beach, then go and see Kizmel."

"………Yes, ma'am."

She removed her hand from my face, then began to walk down the hill.

Volupta covered about as much space as Lectio, the main town of the floor, but it was at least three times as busy.

The moment we passed through the white stucco gates, we were met by lively shouts and enticing smells from the carts, restaurants, and pubs on either side of the main street. I told myself that we'd just eaten that delicious chicken rice and *kaphrao* in Lectio, but that was already six hours ago. The unplanned hunting session had worn us down a bit, and the evening was approaching, so this was a good chance for an early dinner, I supposed.

"Hey, Asuna…"

"Hey, Kirito," she replied. I held up my palm, motioning for her to go first. She blinked and said, "I'm sure the casino is open late. Should we eat first?"

"Open late? It's open twenty-four hours."

"Oh…"

"But I'm with you on eating. What should we get?"

"What's good around here?" she asked for the second time that day.

I had to think about it; in the beta, the majority of the time I spent on the seventh floor was consumed by this town, but I had few memories of the food here. That was because I had been busy ignoring my earlier advice to be "calm and bold," electing instead to be "panicked and cowardly" and generally making a mess of myself.

"Uh, well…I'll let your instinct and knowledge and general luck with food lead the way here, Asuna."

"I'm not sure what that's supposed to mean…But okay, I guess," she murmured, looking skeptical but also a bit pleased with herself.

Because of the slope, the north side of Volupta was uptown, where the homes were, and the south side was downtown, where business occurred. Virtually all the places to eat, however, were located along the main street that ran east to west through the center of the town.

It was also arranged so that the farther you went down the street toward the Volupta Grand Casino, the fancier the places got. The prices the luxury restaurant across the street from the casino charged were absolutely preposterous by the standards of the seventh-floor economy.

Belatedly, I started to panic at the thought of Asuna choosing that place in particular. Fortunately, her white-leather boots came clicking to a stop about a third of the way down the street.

With its wide-open doorway and mix of indoor and outdoor seating, the establishment seemed more like a café than a restaurant. There was much clinking of utensils and glasses coming from the bright interior—and plenty of lively chatter. I didn't mind that kind of atmosphere, but it didn't strike me as Asuna's kind of thing.

"You sure you want this one...?" I asked hesitantly.

A moment later, I heard an especially loud voice shout, "Don't hold back, boys! This one's on me! Order all ya want!"

There were cheers and whistles in response.

"You're a good man!"

"With a spiky head o' hair!"

"Three more large ales over here, ma'am!"

"Make it four!"

"And two sausage assortments!"

Asuna and I shared a look of foreboding, then walked to the entrance and peered inside.

The interior wasn't particularly large, featuring just two tables in the middle. But they were spacious ones, packed with players wearing familiar equipment colored dark iron-gray and moss green. We didn't need to see the guild tag on their cursors. They belonged to one of the two big advancement guilds, the Aincrad Liberation Squad. In the center of the table on the left, chugging a large mug, was their spiky-haired leader, Kibaou. Around him were other principal members of the guild, like Okotan, Schinkenspeck, and Hokkai Ikura.

"How are they already here...?" I muttered.

Asuna sighed. "Were they already on their way here before us...?"

Since they didn't pass us on the Tailwind Road, it was the only possibility. That meant ALS had stayed at an inn in Lectio last night, then left first thing in the morning to get to Volupta.

Lectio was a boring town, it was true, but there were a fair number of quests to do, with some pretty good hunting areas, too. Unlike with a smaller and nimbler guild, it was too easy for the members of a larger guild to start to drift apart in terms of levels. You'd assume they would want to spend an entire day around the first town of a new floor just working on leveling up. So why did they rush out of town at the first opportunity, and why were they carousing here with drinks?

Neither Asuna nor I could answer that question. Just then, there was another cheer from a different group behind us.

"……?"

We turned to look at the other side of the street. There was a restaurant there about the same size, if marginally more elegant. We trotted across the street and peered through the window because the doors were closed.

"To today's victory!" said a voice. It was followed by a chorus roaring, "Cheers!"

Filling the seats around two large tables were a group of players wearing metallic-silver and cobalt-blue clothing. It was clearly the other of the two main guilds, the Dragon Knights Brigade.

Standing alone in the back of the room and raising a mug of ale was a thin man with long hair tied into a ponytail. That was their guild leader, Lind. Nearby were Shivata and Hafner, two of his guildmates.

"The DKB, too…But why…?" Asuna asked.

"And why are they toasting and drinking at this hour?" I wondered.

"He said something about '*today's victory*.' Did they beat a field boss or something?"

"I don't think there were any FBs worth celebrating around Volupta," I said, earning a cold look from Asuna for the lazy abbreviation.

She pulled back from the window. "Well, I would assume that both guilds have come here for the casino, but I can't help but wonder why they chose competing locations right across the street from each other. It would be nice to figure out what's going on, before they wind up dragging us into it."

I had no qualms with that. We'd suffered from the DKB and ALS's battle over the guild flag on the fifth floor, and the race to beat the floor boss on the sixth floor, so if they were butting heads over some new advantage, I wanted to know what was going on before it got out of hand.

That left just one person to consult, of course.

"She's probably here in this town, too. Might as well get in touch," I muttered. Asuna's face lit up as she nodded.

The response to my request to meet in person came two minutes later.

I'M IN A HOT SPOT RIGHT NOW. CAN IT BE IN FIFTEEN MINUTES? I'LL SEE YOU AT A PLACE CALLED POTS 'N' POTS ON THE SOUTH-WEST SIDE OF THE FOUNTAIN SQUARE.

Asuna read the message over my shoulder and wondered, "Hot spot...? Like, for earning experience points?"

"I doubt it's that..."

"Then what is it?"

"You'll have to ask her yourself," I said, closing the window.

The fountain square in question was located where the east-west main street intersected with a grand staircase that went north-south up the hill; it was less than a hundred meters away from our present spot. If we walked straight there, it would take less than five minutes, so we took our time checking out the various places to eat on either side of the road, arriving at the square after another ten minutes.

The plaza was, according to my research, the third-best tourist spot in Volupta, following the casino and the beach. It wasn't all that large, but there was a statue of the bird-headed goddess of luck in the fountain, where pure water flooded out of the natural rock at her feet to form a circular pool around her.

When Asuna got closer and peered through the metal fence around the fountain, she let out a gasp.

"Look! All those gold and silver coins!"

As she said, there were tons of glittering coins at the bottom of the water, shining in the light of the fires all around. If I was remembering correctly, it seemed like there were far more coins than the last time I'd seen it.

"Don't jump in to scoop them up, or the guards will kick you out."

"I'm not going to do that!" she protested, jabbing me in the side. "It's lovely, though…like Trevi Fountain."

"Oh, even I know that one. It's in Rome, right?"

"Correct. I'll throw in a coin, too," said Asuna, pulling two silver coins from a little pocket in her belt pouch.

"What?! You're throwing in two hundred col?! There isn't any buff from this fountain."

"I don't care!"

She glared at me once again, then, for some reason, turned her back to the fountain and tossed the coins in over her shoulder. They splashed in the water and sank, wavering downward until they sat atop the piles on the bottom.

"…You didn't have to throw both of them…"

Two hundred col was enough for five extra-large plates of Min's chicken and rice in Lectio, I thought, frustrated. But Asuna just sighed and explained, "At Trevi Fountain, there's a saying that the number of coins you throw in will change the wish it grants."

"Oh yeah? How so?"

"One coin means you'll be able to come back to Rome. Two coins means you'll be there with that special…"

But she stopped abruptly and clamped her mouth shut, looking away.

"You'll have to look it up on your own to learn the rest."

"How am I going to do that in Aincrad…?"

"Once we're back in the real world, you can do an Internet search or whatever."

"It's going to be a while, then," I said, thinking to myself, *I'm sure I'll have forgotten about it by that point.* Then I glanced at the right corner of my view. "Uh-oh, one more minute!"

"Oh, that's right."

We left the fountain and rushed to the southwest part of the square. There was only a sightseeing-guide area there, however, and no shop called Pots 'n' Pots.

"Hmm, nothing here…Is it on another corner?"

"No. Hang on."

I tugged on the sleeve of Asuna's tunic, my nose twitching. I thought I'd caught a very faint whiff of something tantalizing on the night breeze.

"…This way, I think…?"

I led us south, down the grand staircase through the town. Despite the name, the steps were about ten feet long and thirty feet wide, with flower beds in the middle. It was really more of a street that happened to be made of steps. At the end, ahead of us, was a large gate, with the beach and ocean (lake, technically) just past it, followed by the outer aperture of the floor and the infinite sunset beyond. It was a tremendous view, but now was not the time to admire it.

I headed down the staircase, pulling on Asuna's sleeve all the while, then took her down a narrow side route to the right. Directly behind the sightseeing-guide area from earlier, there was a little sign. In loopy handwriting, it did appear to say *Pots 'n' Pots*, but I didn't know what it was supposed to mean.

"Oh! This is it!" Asuna exclaimed, just as I heard some faint footsteps. A small figure came rushing up to us at high speed from the other end of the alley and came to a stop before we could even react.

"Sorry, sorry. Twenty seconds late!" said the figure, a small player in a sand-gray hooded cape—the info broker, Argo the Rat, bowing.

Asuna yanked her sleeve out of my grasp and took a step forward. "No, it's fine," she said happily. "We just got here ourselves!"

"Ah, I see. It's been a while, A-chan…Or has it? It was only last night, huh?" Argo said with a shrug.

I waved my hand and said, "Hey. Sorry to bother you when you were in your hot spot."

"Nah, it's fine. It was the right place to quit anyway."

"Did you win?"

"A fair bit. I'm only doing a preliminary investigation today."

It was at this point that Asuna awkwardly interrupted, "Ohhh, when you said it was a hot spot, you meant at the casino? Were you betting, Argo?"

"Now, when ya put it that way, it sounds like I was doin' something criminal. Just a little gambling, more like."

"That's the same thing," she said.

Argo grinned and chuckled, then patted Asuna on the elbow. "C'mon, don't be a stick in the mud. I gotta start sellin' the first issue of my seventh-floor strategy guide by the end of the night. It's part of an info broker's job."

Yeah, a likely story, I thought. Still, it gave me an idea.

"Wait…You aren't selling seventh-floor strategy guides yet? I was sure the ALS and DKB came straight to Volupta because they'd already read your work…"

Argo shrugged. "Welp, we ain't the only beta testers. They musta learned about the casino on their end…Hey, you wanna go inside? I'm starving."

The instant she said it, my virtual stomach rumbled. Asuna nodded deeply without a word, so we followed Argo into the mysterious Pots 'n' Pots.

Inside, it was even smaller than the chicken-and-rice place in Lectio, with just four seats at a counter. Three of them went to Argo, Asuna, and me. There was no menu to be found on the counter. I was looking around when I heard a voice from beyond Asuna say, "The menu's on the wall ahead of us, Kii-boy."

"Mwha—?"

I looked up and saw, on the back wall, a board packed with small alphabetical letters. I'd thought it was just decoration initially, but now I could see it was a menu.

"Uhhh…Chicken and tomato…chicken and beans…chicken and mushroom…"

I skipped down a ways and saw that, after chicken, the items were all "beef and something," then "fish and something," then "mutton and something," until you reached the left side, where they finished with rabbit, deer, and partridge.

"I know what rabbit and deer are...but what's partridge?" I wondered.

Fortunately, Asuna had the answer. "It's a kind of bird...In Japanese, we call them mountain quail, if I remember correctly."

"Mountain quail...? How is that different from regular quail?"

"I don't know. Because they live in the mountains?"

"Oh. Makes sense."

I focused on the menu again. There had to be a hundred of the packed names on the list, but the problem was that I had no idea what sort of *dish* they were describing. If I ordered the partridge and beans and got a whole roasted partridge stuffed with beans, I wasn't sure my ravenous appetite would last. I couldn't ask the cook, either, because there was no one behind the counter. What could it mean?

"I'll have beef an' potatoes."

"And I'd like the rabbit and herbs, I think."

After the girls ordered, a voice from somewhere replied, "Sure!"

I jumped up, startled, and leaned over the counter from a standing position. A very short person walked out of a door on the left and stuck something round they were holding with both hands into the oven on the right.

This NPC had to be the proprietor, I assumed. Their large chef's hat fell over their eyes, and the red scarf tied around their neck went up to their ears, so there was no way to tell for sure if they were male or female, young or old. The only thing I could be sure of was that if I didn't give my order, I wasn't going to be getting any dinner.

"Umm...umm...then I'll have...partridge and parsnips!" I said out of sheer abandon. If I didn't know what they were, might as well choose from the bottom. The chef said "Sure!" again and vanished into the darkness of the kitchen on the left, then reemerged with another mysterious round object that went into the oven.

The actual dish itself was still a total mystery, but within a minute, an extremely fragrant and delectable smell filled the little shop, much to my relief. It certainly wasn't a bad smell, and after all, this location had been chosen by the Rat, the greatest info dealer in all of Aincrad. We could trust her taste.

After another minute, the chef pulled two of the round things from the oven, placed them on simple wooden plates, then added a knife, fork, and spoon, and set them in front of Asuna and Argo.

The objects were, in fact, crispy round bread rolls. They looked good…but what happened to the beef and rabbit?

Asuna had figured out the trick, however; she grabbed the bread without hesitation and pulled the top off. A burst of steam issued from inside, and I murmured with admiration. The six-inch bread roll had been hollowed out and filled with a thick brown stew.

"Ahhh, so *that's* what this is…" I murmured.

Asuna gave me a funny look and said proudly, "You should have figured it out from the name."

"Huh? Pots 'n' Pots…? What is it supposed to mean?"

"They're pot roasts in bread bowls."

"Oh…sure…I get it…"

You could have warned me, Rat! I thought, glaring past Asuna. But Argo was already taking a bite out of her bread lid, which she'd dipped into the stew first.

I very nearly started drooling at the sight, so it was fortunate that my own golden-brown bread bowl was placed before me at that moment. Asuna had been considerate enough to wait for my dish to arrive, so we said our grace first, then lifted the bread lid off the top.

Inside the bread roll was a creamy white stew. I copied Argo and split the piece of bread in half, then dipped it into the stew and took a bite.

It was good. It tasted like the cream stew I was used to eating in the real world, but there was a more gamey scent to this one, with a little accent of sweetness. I finished the bread lid very quickly, then picked up my spoon. The first thing to try was the "moun-tain quail" partridge, which had a rich, tender, savory taste. Then

I scooped up a mysterious white ingredient. It was a semicircular piece of something that looked like potato or turnip.

"So this is a parsnip...?" I wondered to myself, giving it an appraising look.

Asuna appeared to be feeling sorry for me. "Did you order that without knowing what it was?"

"Yeah."

"It's lizard's tail."

"...What?"

I immediately held the spoon at arm's length. Of course, everything here—the partridge, Asuna's rabbit, and Argo's deer—were all just digital data, and lizard meat would be no different. But that didn't matter. I had standards, and they mattered to *me*.

"...What kind of combination is quail and lizard...?" I muttered to myself. Asuna and Argo burst into laughter.

"You're amazing, Kii-boy. It's always worth teasing you. That's a vegetable."

"What, really?"

"Yes, really. In Japan, we call it sugar carrot or American parsley," Asuna explained smugly. I gave her a sidelong glance, then popped the white object into my mouth. It had a crisp crunch like a carrot but with its own flavor and sweetness. It was odd, but I didn't mind it.

"Hmm. I can see why they call it sugar carrot," I commented, once I'd swallowed the piece.

"Technically, though, it's a relative of celery," Asuna pointed out.

"......As long as it's not a lizard's tail, I don't care."

With that, I started to eat the dish in earnest. I had only gotten two or three bites in when Argo spoke up.

"Do you two wanna trade?"

Asuna and I shared a look, then we both indicated that we would.

First my bread bowl made its way over to Argo, then Argo's dish went to Asuna, and Asuna's slid over to me. This one was rabbit and herb, if I recalled correctly. The texture was meatier than the partridge, but it didn't have a funny aftertaste, and the blend of herbs gave it a stimulating and complementary flavor.

Once we'd eaten another third of the stews, we slid them over again. Argo's beef and potatoes had that classic, comforting taste. The combination of large, juicy meat and steamy potato was supremely satisfying. Once I'd reached the bottom of the bread bowl, I asked Asuna quietly, "Are we allowed to eat the bread it's in, too?"

"Why not? We've got knives."

"Ohhh, it's for cutting the bread…"

I picked up the serrated knife and sliced the empty bread bowl in two, then into smaller pieces. I popped one of the stew-soaked bits into my mouth. I was happily chewing away while Asuna cut hers into more manageable pieces. She asked, "Which was your favorite stew, Kirito?"

"Uhhh…Well, they were all good. The mountain quail and lizard—er, sugar carrot—was new and interesting. The rabbit and herb was bold and stimulating, while the beef and potato was safe and delicious…But if I had to choose one as the winner, I guess I'd go with the rabbit."

"Oh really? Why?"

"I think I liked the texture best."

"Hmm, interesting…"

I wasn't sure what exactly she found "interesting," but she nodded anyway and stuck her fork into one of the neatly cut squares of bread.

Once we were done, we left the building. Volupta was in night mode now. I inhaled the soothing breeze coming up from the beach and stretched luxuriously.

"Ahhh, that was good…Thanks for showing us this place, Argo."

"Right outside the square isn't where you'd think ta look, huh? I'll give ya that one for free."

"Hey, thanks," I said with a grimace.

Asuna suddenly gasped. "Oh!"

"Wh-what is it?"

"...I feel like we weren't contacting Argo to catch dinner with her."

The Rat and I both gasped, too. "Oh!"

We'd just paid for the meal at Pots 'n' Pots and left, so it would be embarrassing to go back inside. But it felt like a waste of time to go searching for a café to sit in, too. Instead, we decided to register at an inn.

The inns of Volupta were clustered on the south side of town, closer to the beach, but the finest place of all was upstairs at the casino. We'd need casino chips to stay there, though, rather than col.

So we strolled down the great stairs, turning right when we reached the fancy gate at the bottom, which was guarded by watchmen. Once you were this close to the beach, you couldn't actually see it anymore, because of the tall stone walls blocking access.

"...I wonder if the people who live here complain about the fact that the beach is exclusively for tourists who gamble at the casino," Asuna murmured. I was going to say that they were just NPCs but decided against it.

Kizmel the dark elf wasn't the only NPC we'd met who had advanced conversational skills and emotional intelligence on the level of a human being; Myia, Theano, and Bouhroum were recent examples of the same on the sixth floor. Not all NPCs were like that, but somewhere in Volupta were probably some NPCs with the same level of artificial intelligence.

I'd prefer not to see any NPCs die on this floor, I thought, just as Argo answered Asuna's question.

"Mmm, they might. The whole town's more or less ruled over by that gigantic casino."

"R-ruled over? That sounds ominous..."

"There are company towns in the real world, too, right? Volupta's economy is run by the tourists who come for the casino, so the residents can't really complain that they close off the beach."

Asuna glanced up at the stone wall to the left. "When you put it that way…I'd almost feel bad about the idea of relaxing and having fun on the beach…"

"Uh-huh? So you two are after the beach, huh? Well, now I feel bad for sayin' that."

"No, actually. I'm glad you told us," Asuna admitted. I watched her closely and asked, "So uh…should we forget about the beach?"

"Mmm…no," she said, to my surprise. "On the sixth floor, we learned that this world often doesn't work the way its background suggests it should. I've decided to make up my mind based on what I see and hear for myself. And that means ignoring what you've just told us, unfortunately."

"Nee-hee-hee, no worries. I always gotta be on my toes so I don't just swallow everything I hear through the grapevine, too. Oh…my recommendation is *this* place," Argo said, pointing at a four-story inn up ahead. She grinned and added, "But of course, A-chan'll want to check it out for herself before she decides to stay there."

4

ARGO'S RECOMMENDATION, THE AMBERMOON INN, was met with Asuna's approval as soon as she walked inside.

The DKB and ALS were already here in force, so I was worried we might have trouble finding a room, but either they were putting off getting their lodgings for the night, or they were planning to stay at the casino's luxury hotel. All the rooms here were available.

Argo was going to stay here, too, so we decided to go for a platinum suite for the three of us. The price was thrilling in its extravagance, but split three ways, it wasn't unaffordable. Naturally, there were three rooms in the suite, so I wasn't worried about any situations beyond the capabilities of an eighth-grade boy, like what happened in the dark elf camp on the third floor, or Castle Galey on the sixth floor. This arrangement should be fine. *Should be.*

There was no elevator, so we had to schlep up the stairs to the fourth floor. Asuna opened the door—locked by an ordinary key, not a puzzle—then said "It's amazing!" the moment she stepped inside.

I found out what was amazing about it at once. The walls across the spacious common room had three large windows, a rare style in Aincrad. It gave a panoramic view of the beach and water at the south edge of town.

The sun was already down, but there were torches lit at regular intervals along the beach, and the moonlight coming through the outer aperture cast a pale stripe across the surf. The furnishings in the room weren't up to the standard set by the dark elf castle, but the view was easily top two among all the places we'd stayed.

Asuna rushed to the window to take in the night view. The sight of her framed against that background was like a work of art. I just gazed at the scene, taking it in, until I felt like someone was staring at me.

"…Whatcha grinnin' at?"

"Uh, nothing."

Argo hissed with laughter and removed her hooded cape, then walked over to the kitchen space in the corner of the living room. In the real world, there would be a refrigerator with cold drinks inside, but Aincrad didn't have any condensers or ice magic. If you lit a stove, you could boil water for tea, but it was still a midsummer's kind of night, if not quite as hot as the day. I didn't want anything hot to drink.

"I'll just have some of the water, Argo," I said, walking over to pour it myself, but Argo snatched the pitcher away.

"Just leave this to Big Sis."

She put the pitcher and three glasses on a tray, then took it over to the sofas in the center of the living room. I had no choice but to follow her, so I helped set the glasses on the low table, then sat down on the soft cushions.

"C'mere, A-chan. You'll like this," said Argo. Asuna turned around at last, blinking as though broken out of a spell. She sat next to me, looking curious.

"I'll like…what?"

"Just watch."

Argo filled the three glasses with water, then opened her inventory window. She produced a pale-blue nut…no, a flower bud? It was a rounded object, less than three quarters of an inch, pointed on one end. I couldn't remember seeing this in the beta test.

Argo dropped the blue bud in one of the glasses. It sank at

first, then slowly rose back up, making faint fizzing and cracking sounds.

When the finely frothing bud reached the surface again, it gently broke apart. Delicate, translucent petals expanded, and the cracking grew louder.

Five seconds later, the flower was completely open. It was beautiful but had a strange shape. There were six hexagonal petals pointing in six directions, while the center was shaped like a twenty-sided die, complete with triangular faces. As I watched, spellbound, it grew more and more translucent. It was closer to a fine ice sculpture than a plant.

"It's beautiful..." Asuna murmured, suddenly leaning forward. She peered directly down the top of the glass, then smiled and said, "I knew it."

"You knew what?"

"Look at it from this angle."

When I followed Asuna's lead, I gasped. The ice flower was identical to a snowflake crystal from above. I glanced across the table, still crouching, and asked the grinning info dealer, "What *is* this, Argo?"

"Oh, we're not even at the surprise yet. Take a drink, A-chan."

"Uh, okay..."

The moment her outstretched fingertips touched the glass, she exclaimed, "It's cold!" The sides of the glass were already beading up with tiny droplets.

She grabbed the glass firmly this time and held it up. Summoning her courage, she pressed it to her mouth. The flower on the surface wavered and clinked against the side.

Asuna took a small sip first to test, then kept going, drinking half the glass. She pulled away and looked from me to Argo.

"It's cold! It's great! It's *cold*!"

"W-wow, really? Let me try..." I asked, reaching out, but Argo interrupted.

"Look, Kii-boy, I got one for you, too."

She had already prepared ice flowers for the other two glasses. She pushed one to me, which I grabbed, feeling shocked at the stabbing chill in my palm. It was practically cold enough to stick to my skin. I poured the liquid down my throat.

It was pure ice water. There was a little hint of mint flavor, which only added to the pure taste of the liquid. The chilled water flooded down my throat, and the effect it had upon my sunbaked body was indescribably pleasurable.

I quaffed down two-thirds of the glass all at once, then exhaled with satisfaction. I hadn't had any ice water in Aincrad since Yofel Castle on the fourth floor. It was cold enough to snow back then, so it didn't hit quite the same. Here on the seventh floor, which was as hot as summer, that ice water was even better than a powerful healing potion.

"Argo…what's this flower called?" I asked again.

The Rat took a mouthful of the water before answering. "The item name is Snow Tree Bud. Its effect, as you can see, is to chill a single glass of water. When you're done, it conveys two buffs."

"Huh? Really?"

"You think I'd lie about it? By the way, you gotta drink all the water before the ice flower completely melts, or ya don't get the buff."

"Huh? Really?" I repeated, staring down the top of the glass. The snowflake-patterned flower did seem to be smaller than when it first bloomed.

I wanted to sip and savor the drink, but I was curious about that buff, too. Tense, I tilted the bottom of the glass higher. The chill from the ice water flowing down my throat paralyzed me with refreshment. I watched my HP bar as I drank, and a second later, two small icons appeared. One was the familiar sign for gradual HP regeneration, while the other was a combination of a shield and a small flame.

"Oh…Is this a flame-resistance buff?"

"Yes." Argo grinned. I stared at the icons, then at her.

"Hang on. Healing is nice, but flame resistance is a very rare benefit. Why are you just giving it to us for fun in here?"

"Don't worry about it. I got plenty."

"Wh-where did you find them?"

"Well, *there's* a nugget I'm not gonna let slip for free."

You're killing me! I wanted to shout. But she was an intelligence broker, after all. If anything, I ought to be grateful for what she had told me for free already.

"…Uh…how much?" I asked, dreading the answer.

Argo lifted her glass with both hands; she still had plenty of water left. "Hmmmm," she considered. "Well, I could go ahead and charge you a simple col price…but instead, I'd rather take payment in labor."

"L-labor?"

I turned to share a look with my partner—except that Asuna wasn't looking at me; she was staring at the ice flower in her empty glass. So I looked back at Argo again.

"What kind of labor are you looking for…?"

"Don't be scared. Would I put you and A-chan in danger? I just want a little help with a quest that's tough for a single person to tackle."

"A quest…"

It was true that there were many quests in *SAO* that were basically impossible to complete on your own. They had been a source of great frustration to me in the beta. All I needed to do was recruit some brief party members, but if it were that easy for me to do, I'd be aligned with one of the two big guilds by now.

In that sense, it was a mystery to me why Asuna, who had at least ten times the social communication skills that I did, had spent an entire month playing solo. But I felt like part of that reason was the massive imbalance between men and women in the frontline group as a whole. It had been two months since the deadly game started, and the DKB and ALS had only a handful of women between them. There was no difference in skill, so

I had to assume that the exclusionary atmosphere around the group was driving female players away. It was going to take a female leader to change that…

I shook my head to dispel that train of thought and focused on Argo's face.

"If there's a quest you can't beat alone in this town, it has to be at the casino, right?"

"Brilliant deduction…Okay, not that brilliant. There's barely a single quest in Volupta that doesn't involve the casino in some way."

"Hmm. Well, I could help…but I'd rather not get involved in another epic-length quest series like the 'Curse of Stachion' on the last floor."

"Don't worry; it's a real quickie…I assume."

That does not sound reassuring, I thought, glancing aside again. Asuna was still staring at the bottom of her glass.

"…Um…Asuna?" I asked quietly, drawing the fencer's attention at last. She looked to me, then Argo, then asked bashfully, "Argo, is it okay to eat this flower?"

"It looks tasty, huh? Go right ahead," she said, assuring her. My curiosity was piqued, too.

I picked up the ice flower, which had melted down to bite size at the bottom of the glass, and popped it into my mouth, crunching the delicate structure. It gave off more of that pleasant minty flavor. I placed the empty glass back onto the table.

Asuna and I thanked her for the treat, agreed to help with her request, and then, finally, I was ready to explain the reason we got in touch with her.

"So…we didn't meet up with you to eat good food or get a better rate on a nice hotel room. It's because we saw the ALS and DKB already in town, having competing feasts in the middle of the afternoon, and we wanted to know why."

"Wha—? Really? That's all?" Argo said, sinking deeper into the leather sofa.

I narrowed my eyes. "Well, it's not natural, is it? I would understand if the ALS members were doing it, but the DKB is the more serious of the two. And they were toasting with mugs and everything."

"Oh yeah? Wish I coulda seen it. But if they were havin' feasts here, there's obviously only one reason," Argo said breezily. She glanced at the ceiling. "It's not really worth holdin' over your head, so I'll consider the cost included in the other matter we just negotiated. They were toasting because they won big at the casino."

"Huh?" I muttered—as did Asuna. "They won big...as in, they were gambling the moment they got to Volupta?!"

"They were having a toast because they won big?!"

The two of us were surprised in slightly different ways, but neither question seemed to bother Argo.

"That's right. I'm not just imaginin' that, either. I saw 'em carryin' on, myself."

"What did they win at? You can't make a killing on cards or dice or roulette in half a day."

"......You sound like you understand too much about that," Asuna said, her gaze piercing my left cheek. I did my best to ignore it, awaiting Argo's answer.

For some reason, the information agent grinned and held up her index finger. "Well, I didn't know until I went inside that they've changed a bunch of stuff since the beta."

"In what way?"

"The biggest change is that the main event happens twice, both in the day and at night."

I sucked in a breath, knowing that Asuna would not understand what Argo was talking about.

"......Really...?"

I leaned back, sinking into the plush sofa. Asuna jabbed at my left arm.

"What is it? What main event?"

"Uhhh..."

I carefully did not meet her eye as I described the particular gambling attraction that caused me to lose everything but my sword in the beta test.

"The Battle Arena...It's a monster coliseum."

5

WE CLEANED UP THE DISHES ON THE TABLE, THEN washed off the dust and sweat of the day in the suite's bath. Not all at once, of course; I went first, followed by Asuna and Argo. Although I finished my bath in just three minutes, the girls took over thirty, which was long enough for me to gain a point in my Meditation skill while waiting.

I'd gained the Meditation skill from Bouhroum, the old man with the hamburg steak in Castle Galey on the sixth floor, but it was still largely a mystery to me. The effect of Meditation itself was simple—if you maintained a kind of Zen meditation pose for a certain period of time, you gained an HP regeneration buff and a mild resistance to all negative status ailments. It was a very useful thing, but when you started at zero proficiency, it took sixty seconds of Zen meditation to go into effect. That wasn't viable in battle.

On the other hand, I couldn't have counteracted the paralyzing throwing darts of the Fallen Elves who attacked Castle Galey without the Meditation effect. It was going to be a crucial skill when I knew I was going up against them again—or certain PKers who used similar weapons. That was all fine and good; the problem was the Awakening mod on the Meditation skill.

Skill mods were extra effects you could earn at certain milestones for each skill, and normally they were very easy to understand. For weapon skills, you had things like Sword Skill Cooldown Reduction and Critical Rate Increase. For the Search skill, you got effects like Increased Simultaneous Tracking and Search Distance Increased. In most cases, you didn't even need a description.

But the name Awakening didn't tell you anything. Even the description only said: FOCUSES CONCENTRATION TO THE EXTREME AND DRAWS OUT HIDDEN STRENGTH. The thought of using up a valuable skill slot just for the sake of this mystery mod gave me pause, but Awakening was a mod that was only available at a Meditation skill proficiency of 500, so if I took Meditation out of its slot now, I would probably never see it again.

I had some ideas about what Awakening might do, however.

At the very end of the fight against the Irrational Cube, the boss of the sixth floor, a PKer named Buxum made his move. He snuck up behind the nearly dead boss, pulled out the golden cube that had Break and Bind powers, then used them to freeze every last player in the chamber aside from himself.

When I saw Buxum about to kill Myia's mother, Theano, I screamed at myself to "move" with all the willpower I had, feeling the neurons burning in my brain. That was when I saw, next to the paralysis icon, a new buff icon that looked similar to Meditation. It was a person in a Zen pose, with a ring of golden light in the background.

The moment that icon appeared, my freezing debuff was gone, and I charged at Buxum. I sliced through his longsword and arm with a simple swing, not even a sword skill. Unfortunately, he managed to escape, but if I hadn't broken through the debuff, not only would Myia and Theano be dead, but probably Asuna and I would be, too.

Was that the effect of the Awakening mod? Had I "focused to the extreme" and "drawn out hidden strength" to break the curse of the golden cube?

But Aincrad was just a VR world generated by the NerveGear.

There were no real miracles or magic spells in this world, so how would they measure something immeasurable like "concentration"? Was Akihiko Kayaba's NerveGear somehow capable of not only receiving the brain's movement commands to manipulate the avatar—but reading a person's thoughts as well?

And speaking of mysteries, Buxum's identity was one, too. He wore a sallet helmet that covered everything from his nose on upward, so I couldn't make out his facial features, but if he'd been undercover in the DKB, the rest of his guild must have seen his face. The DKB and ALS held an emergency meeting in the boss chamber about him after the fight, but I still hadn't heard what came of that discussion. I was thinking I'd have to drop Shivata a line about that as the girls emerged from the other room.

Asuna wore a puffy-sleeved mini one-piece with leggings that went down past the knee, while Argo had a very odd look by her standards, with a simple sleeveless shirt and shorts. I couldn't help but stare. It put the biggest smirk I'd ever seen on Argo's face.

"What's up, Kii-boy? Entranced by Big Sis's beautiful legs?"

"I-I'm not entranced by anything!" I shot back, sounding like a fourth grader. Then I added, "I was just thinking, that must be nice to wear."

"Then why don't you change into something more summery?" Asuna pointed out immediately. I looked at my outfit.

I'd taken off the coat and breastplate, so I was only wearing a black long-sleeve shirt and black pants now. It was anything but "summery." However, the Skintight Shirt's material was thin, and the Trousers of Shadowthread were a rare drop—and very breathable, considering how good their defense was. But the most important thing of all was…

"…If I take these off, I'll be in my underwear."

Asuna's eyebrows shot upward. "Nobody asked you to strip! I said, why don't you *change!*"

"Uhhh, but I don't have any other clothes to wear…"

Asuna and Argo exchanged a knowing look and then shared a heavy sigh. I could practically hear them thinking, *Boys...*

Fortunately, they didn't bug me about clothes after that. Instead, we went down to the first floor and headed outside.

It was after eight o'clock. That was usually when the night session of game play began, but we had no plans to leave town tonight. I assumed I wouldn't need my sword, but just in case, I kept my backup shortsword equipped at my left side, rather than gathering virtual dust in my inventory.

The coastal street greeted us with a tropical scent. From there, we walked leisurely up one of the three staircase streets, the western staircase. It was only half as wide as the great stairs, but there were sketchy-looking item shops and pubs along the way, giving it a real "RPG back alley" vibe.

I recalled that a number of quests started here, but we ignored them all as we climbed the worn steps. Eventually, a very large and brightly illuminated building came into view.

Minarets split the night sky above its navy-blue dome. Three-point flags of red and black snapped in the breeze. That was the Volupta Grand Casino, a place of joy and despair.

I suddenly noticed that despite the cooling temperature, both of my palms were slick with sweat. I almost played along with the trope and muttered "Am I...actually afraid...?" but I figured the girls would either not get the reference or think I was being stupid.

From the western staircase, we headed into the plaza in front of the casino, where things looked dramatically different. It was a little bit smaller than the square at the center of the town with the fountain, but the tiles underfoot were arranged in detailed and complex mosaics, and the businesses lining the sides were very refined. The most stunning part of all, however, was the stateliness of the casino on the west end of the square. Its white walls were lit by torches, and the pillars were carved into statues that made it look like the home of a king.

In fact, it truly *was* the castle of Volupta. Whoever owned the Grand Casino—I didn't know their name or face—was indeed the ruler of this town.

Armed guards stood on either side of the open entrance, through which came the light sound of string music and lively chatter from the dazzling interior. All the NPCs walking inside were dressed in their best clothes. When Asuna noticed them, she leaned over and whispered, "Hey, this casino doesn't have a dress code, does it?"

"Dress code...?"

At first, I thought she was talking about a code for a DLC (downloadable content) item or something, since she'd used the English term. When I realized she was talking about clothing standards, I waved my hand and shook my head. "No, not at all. I'm sure they'd stop you if you were wearing only underwear, but they don't care if you're in your starter gear, or a tattered robe, or full plate armor. You think those slobs in the DKB and ALS have formal wear?"

"...That's a good point," said Asuna, buying the explanation immediately.

It was like a summoning spell. No sooner had I mentioned them than I heard a grating, familiar Kansai accent from the other side of the square.

"Awright, let's win the jackpot and take home that big-ass sword!"

Others replied to his announcement with grunts like "Yeah!" and "You bet!" We quickly backed away and hid under the eaves of one of the businesses so we could watch the east side of the square.

Walking down the main street was a group of about ten players wearing dark green and iron black. We didn't need to see the spiky hair of the man leading them to recognize the ALS. Apparently they had finished their guild feast, and now the senior members were heading into the casino to enjoy their evening.

Kibaou's group stomped across the square, with no sign that

they were aware we were even there, and went through the casino entrance. They were probably planning to bet big on the Battle Arena that would be starting again at nine.

"…What big-ass sword?" I wondered. I couldn't remember anything like that during the beta. Argo just shrugged and whispered back, "Go and see for yerself."

"Fine…Well, let's go," I said, pulling off of the wall—but Asuna pushed me back. Before I could protest, I heard approaching footsteps.

Another group, about the same size but in dark blue and silver, took the exact same route as the ALS. In the lead was Lind, the calligraphy club member; to his right was Shivata, the track-and-field runner, and to his left was Hafner, the soccer player. It was the DKB, the other major guild. Their descriptions weren't actually true, just epithets I used, but I didn't have room to be insulting, really. Other players kept calling me nicknames like Master Black, so it was about time I helped their nicknames catch on among the group, too.

In the meantime, Lind's group crossed the square and disappeared into the casino, too. There was no question they were heading for the night installment of the Battle Arena, just like Kibaou's gang.

"…How many chips did they win at the arena during the day…?" I muttered to myself, but I didn't expect Argo to actually answer me.

"I checked up on that. Apparently they both got over a thousand."

"A thou…"

I had to clamp my mouth shut to keep from screaming. Instead, my throat worked itself out, and I said quietly, "In that case, they should quit while they're ahead…Wasn't the grand prize at the casino a thousand chips anyway?"

"Plus, they could get a beach pass," said Asuna with no small amount of envy.

Argo looked at both of us and smirked. "Sorry, but your info's old. If you want VIP status and the beach pass that comes with it, you gotta win *thirty* thousand chips."

"Thir...ty..." Asuna gasped.

Then Argo looked at me and dropped another bombshell. "And the highest-value prize got updated, too. You'll need a hundred thousand chips for that one."

"Hun...dred..." I gasped. In the beta, I gambled for the chance to win a thousand chips and ruined myself. To win a hundred times that much—with each chip converting to a hundred col—would require winnings equal to ten million col.

"Ten million? That's ten mega-col...Are they really going to bring out mega items on the seventh floor? And do Lind and Kiba think they're gonna turn a thousand chips into a hundred thousand?" I murmured, feeling light-headed.

Argo just tossed her hands up. "I suppose so. Well, they turned a hundred into a thousand at the daytime coliseum."

"But even then, that's just a tenfold profit...This would be a hundredfold on top of that."

"A hundredfold is just tenfold times tenfold," she said pointlessly.

Asuna crossed her hands in front of her face, then swung them outward in a decisive gesture. "No way! Thirty thousand chips just for the chance to hang out at the beach for half a day? Three million col! That's insane! I mean, that's six million col for the two us—and nine million if we include Argo! If we had that much money, we could just buy an entire house facing the sea!"

"...Again, technically a lake."

"Whatever— Shut up! My point is: no casino! Never mind! Let's go to the next town already!" Asuna fumed and started to walk away, but I pinched her puffy sleeve in a hurry.

"Er, w-wait a sec. We don't have to bet, but we *do* have to fulfill Argo's request."

"......Oh."

She came to a stop. Argo grinned at her. "Don'cha wanna know how to get a Snow Tree Bud, A-chan?"

"………Urrrr…"

She hummed longer than usual, then turned to Argo.

"What do you want us to do?"

Argo simply said "I'll explain inside" and started toward the casino, so we had to follow her bouncing curls.

The entrance to the Volupta Grand Casino was diagonal across the tile mosaics. The huge marble facade was like a five-star hotel's in the real world. Even the shining armor of the guards had been upgraded several levels since the beta.

But Argo was not intimidated in the slightest. Her leather sandals clip-clopped through the doorway. As soon as we passed through after her, we were met with refreshing cool air, then pleasant string music and the smell of sweet flowers.

It was blindingly bright inside the entrance hall, thanks mainly to the massive chandelier. I wondered how many candles and how much oil they used every single night, but there was no point to worrying about that in a virtual world. A statue of a bird-headed goddess stood in the center of the octagonal hall, just like in the fountain square. Behind her was a set of three large doors that headed into the playroom. A staircase on the right wall led upstairs, and the stairs on the left wall descended. The way down was open, but a red rope and an NPC in black blocked the stairs going up. It seemed like the musical performance was floating down from there.

"…What's up there?" Asuna asked.

Argo said, "If it's the same as the beta, the second floor's the high-roller room for VIPs, and the third floor's the luxury hotel. Even I don't know what's on the fourth. You, Kii-boy?"

"Nope," I said, shaking my head.

Asuna shrugged lightly. "Well, it doesn't matter, since we're not gambling. Anyway…Where are we picking up this quest you want us to help you with?"

"Not so fast, A-chan. Even if yer not playing, you can still enjoy the atmosphere," Argo said with a grin and started off again. She made her way around the goddess statue and toward the three doors in the back.

As soon as we passed through the open doorway, the refined string music was too quiet to hear, drowned out by an enthusiastic clamor.

The playroom was about as big as a high school gym. There were countless tables, packed with visitors enjoying games of chance and skill. They were arranged in a three-sided manner that was open toward us, with roulette on the right, dice on the left, and cards taking up the majority of the space straight ahead. This arrangement, at least, was the same as I remembered it being in the beta.

In the middle of the room was the exchange counter, where you could pay col to receive casino chips, and the prize counter where you could trade those chips for items. There were two more bars where you could order drinks and light food, making four counters in the shape of a square. I leaned over to speak to my temporary partner, who was standing in stunned silence.

"Hey, let's just go see what you can win. Don't you want to know what you can get for a hundred thousand chips?"

Asuna blinked several times and looked at me with renewed caution. "Yes...but you'd better not announce you're going to start betting in the hopes of winning it."

"Nope, not gonna. C'mon, let's go," I said, pushing her toward the counters. Argo tagged along, smirking at us.

I glanced at the sides of the room as we walked, and it seemed that most of the gamblers—in fact, all of them—were NPCs. There wasn't a single green cursor in sight to indicate a player. If this were the main town of the floor, they would be flowing through the teleport square from below in the hopes of winning a fortune, but there was a reasonable amount of danger in traveling from Lectio to Volupta. Only the guilds involved with pushing our progress forward would be able to get here on the first day.

That thought made me realize that the DKB and ALS weren't in here, either. They must have gone straight down the stairs in the entrance hall, then. It was currently 8:30. There was still plenty of time before the night arena.

No, no, no! I told myself, cutting off the temptation. I took a right around the exchange counter, passing the bar along the side in order to see the prize counter in the back.

A pillar of marble nearly three meters across, with a splendid display case fixed to it, stood behind a woman in a black vest. There had to be five times as many different items as what they featured in the beta.

On the bottom shelf were the consumable items like potions, which could be won for just a few chips. The shelf above it had useful-looking tools, the one above that had colorful accessories and small pieces of equipment, and on the top shelf, shining brilliantly in the light from the chandelier, was a longsword.

The wide blade was as silver as a mirror, with gold embedded into the bevel line. The brim was golden, too, while the grip was red leather, and a massive jewel adorned the pommel.

"Oof, that's certainly attention-grabbing," Asuna murmured, which I had to agree with. The real issue was its specs. If that sword cost a hundred thousand chips, meaning ten million col, I couldn't begin to imagine what sort of attack power it offered.

I took two steps toward the exchange counter and rose onto tiptoes to see the sword. But you had to tap it with your finger to see the properties window, and there was no way I could do that when the sword was on display over twice my height off the ground.

I had risen up and down off my heels several times when Argo finally noted, "Uh, Kii-boy, you can just get a prize pamphlet at the counter."

"Y-you could have told me first," I grumbled, clearing my throat in embarrassment and taking two more steps up to the counter. The NPC woman gave me a very pleasant and professional smile.

I said "Pamphlet, please!" and she produced a rolled parchment for me, with nary a nasty look at my casual clothing.

"Here you are, sir."

"Thanks," I said, hurrying off to the side to open it up. Asuna peered over my right arm.

It was quite a hefty pamphlet, complete with detailed color illustrations. They didn't have printing technology in this world, which meant—if you really wanted to go down this rabbit hole— that each illustration was painted by hand. But of course, all this was just the magic of games at work.

Below each illustration, the item names were written in the English alphabet, but fortunately for me, the description text was in Japanese. I passed by the potions, tools, and accessories and went to the back of the pamphlet to check out the gold-and-silver-and-jeweled sword.

The illustration was adorned with the name SWORD OF VOLUPTA. To the right of that, it said 100,000 VC. I remembered that VC was the abbreviation of the official name of the Grand Casino's chips, Vol Coins. I'd believed Argo the first time, of course, but actually seeing that number on the page made my head swim.

I shook it to clear my mind and examined the text instead. It said: THE SWORD OF THE HERO FALHARI, FOUNDER OF VOLUPTA AND SLAYER OF THE WATER DRAGON ZARIEGHA. IT HEALS THE WIELDER, PURIFIES ALL POISONS, AND STRIKES TRUE WITH EVERY SWING.

"Hmmmm," I murmured, just as Asuna went, "Rrrmm…"

"It's hard to say what its properties are," she muttered. "It sounds very impressive, but unless we can see an actual readout of its specs…"

I pointed toward the counter. "Asuna, if I let you stand on my shoulders, would you try tapping that sword?"

"Absolutely not."

She wasn't just being a stick in the mud, though; the moment we crossed the space behind the counter, those hardy men dressed in black would come for us. I returned to the text.

"...Based on this, we don't know the actual attack power or the number of upgrade attempts it has, but if the additional effects are exactly as the text suggests, I can see why it would be worth ten million col. Equipping it automatically regenerates HP, nullifies damaging and paralyzing poison, and turns every attack into a critical hit, right?"

Saying it out loud really made clear what an absolutely broken item the Sword of Volupta was; it wasn't meant to exist here, on just the seventh floor. I looked back at the sword on the top shelf of the display case.

The gaudy, eye-catching design wasn't my style, to be sure, but in our circumstances, appearance was hardly the most important thing. If it increased the chances of survival for my partner and me, I'd use a sword a hundred times uglier than that one.

Or so I told myself, at least. For now, this sword was out of reach, both literally and figuratively. If I converted all my assets into chips, I'd have only nine hundred. To turn them into a hundred thousand, I'd have to bet everything double on the roulette wheel and win seven times in a row. The odds of that were...

"...Asuna, what's point-five to the seventh power?"

"Huh? Umm...like, zero-point-zero-zero-seven-eight-humde-dumde-dum...Right?"

"Thanks. So that would be about point-eight percent," I murmured. The fencer looked at me suspiciously for about two seconds, then her brows shot upward.

"Oh! You were asking for the chances of winning seven straight all-or-nothing bets!"

"Uh, yeah. Wow, you figured that out?"

"Of course I did! And you know there's no way a point-eight percent chance will work out!"

"L-look, you don't lose anything just thinking about it."

"But next you'll be saying '*I'm just betting a hundred col*'!" she shot back.

Stifled laughter met our bickering. I glanced over at the Rat, whose painted whiskers were twitching. She cackled and giggled, writhing back and forth for at least five seconds before she finally looked up.

"I tell ya...I never get bored watchin' you two. Please, you gotta stick together for as long as possible."

"Well...we don't have any plans to break it up," I admitted, stone-faced.

"As long as *someone* doesn't bankrupt us at the casino," Asuna added.

We left the gaming room while I still had my willpower intact and returned to the entrance hall. It was 8:40 PM now.

I tossed the pamphlet into my inventory so it would stop tempting me and leaned over to ask Argo, "So...what did you want us to do?"

"Ah, right, right, right."

She snapped her fingers and went through her menu with blinding speed. A party request appeared, and Asuna and I accepted it. A third HP bar appeared in the upper-left corner.

"Now we should be able to share the quest. This way," she said, heading for the descending staircase toward the first basement level. *That's a bad direction to go*, I thought, but I couldn't argue with the client.

The scarlet-carpeted stairs took us along the octagonal walls three-quarters of the way around the first basement hall. There was another statue in the center of the room, but this was not of a bird-headed goddess but a powerful, lion-headed warrior, standing atop another warrior with a lizard head. Beyond the statue was another set of three doors like above, but it was rather dark beyond it.

So here I am again, I grumbled, following Argo through the doors into the Battle Arena.

Excited voices drowned out the faint string music. The wide room was full of a different kind of enthusiasm than in the gaming room above.

It was lowered in the middle like a bowl, and on the far side was a stage covered by a huge golden cage. Buffet tables with bearing finger foods lined the walls on either side of us, and we saw a ticket counter in one corner.

Between the sides of the stage and the buffet tables, there were over fifty guests present, but I couldn't make out their faces in the gloom. Instead, I focused on their silhouettes long enough to bring up the player cursors, one by one.

"...Ah, there's the ALS," I murmured, just as Asuna whispered, "Found DKB."

We indicated the locations to each other with our glances. The ALS members were on the right side of the arena, while the DKB took up spots at the buffet on the left. Both groups had large papers spread out on their table and were deep in excited discussion.

"...I wonder what they're looking at."

"Those are the odds," I explained. "They list the names and descriptions of the monsters that are going to fight on the stage, along with the payout if they win. You can get that free from the ticket counter."

"I don't want them," Asuna claimed, fixing me with an uncomfortably firm glare.

"R-right, of course not. Anyway...Hey, Argo, where's the quest NPC? I don't see any marks."

We were now in a party together, so any ongoing quest NPCs should have had a *!* mark above their head, even if only Argo had picked up the quest. But no amount of searching turned up any sight of one.

"Of course ya don't; the quest NPC's somewhere else," Argo said, turning to me.

"Huh?" I squawked. "Then why are we here?"

"We're runnin' an errand, obviously."

"......"

As a general rule, quests in *SAO* fell into four broad categories.

There were collection quests that involved gathering materials out in the wilderness; combat quests requiring you to defeat a particular monster; escort quests where you helped an NPC get from one place to another safely; and errand quests, which came in a great variety of forms. Errands got called fetch quests for good reason, because many of them involved getting some item and bringing it back—or delivering an item to someone else. But if that's what the quest was, there would need to be a quest NPC to receive the item or give it to us here. And since there was no such NPC...

"Is it...a search? Or an investigation?"

"Yep," said Argo as we walked. I groaned in dismay.

Search and investigation quests were the most troublesome of errands. The "Curse of Stachion" quest on the sixth floor took us all over the place, and it started with a request to find the golden cube. While not everything that happened in it was scripted, it had lasted all the way to the floor boss battle. Praying that this wasn't going to be a similarly epic quest, I asked, "Do we need to find something that someone lost in here?"

"Nope."

"Looking for a person?"

"Nope."

Argo walked down the stairs that went through the lowered part of the floor, cutting down every suggestion I had. When we reached the bottom, she led us right into the ring of NPCs huddled around the battle cage, the covered stage.

The upper-class NPCs lounged on sofas on higher levels that you had to pay for or watched from the buffet tables. The ones gathered directly around the battle cage were rougher, lower-class men. "Whaddaya want?" they grumbled. "Don't push." But Argo ignored them and walked right up to the golden cage, then looked at Asuna and me.

"Ten minutes until the first match. I've got time to explain what I want yer help with."

She beckoned me closer, and I leaned my left ear toward her face. Asuna leaned in with her right ear, putting the two of us face-to-face at a very close distance, but it would be too awkward to change stances now. Fortunately, Asuna didn't seem to mind, so I put on a poker face and listened to Argo's explanation.

"In a few minutes, two monsters are gonna fight inside this cage."

"Yeah."

"According to my quest client, one of them is cheatin' somehow."

"Huh?" I said, louder than I needed to. Both girls put a finger to my lips. I turned my internal volume knob a bit to the left and continued, "Cheating...? These are monsters that are fighting, not humans. Do they even have enough intelligence to cheat...?"

"A kobold or shrewman might, don't you think?" Asuna pointed out.

I shrugged. "Unless things have changed since the beta, there aren't any demihuman monsters in the arena. Probably because it would feel a little too unsavory..."

"They weren't in the daytime arena," Argo agreed, pulling out a piece of folded parchment from her shorts pocket. It was the odds list from the ticket counter. When had she picked that up?

"Here, it's got the first matchup listed."

Asuna and I took the paper and stuck our heads together to read it. Argo pointed to a spot that contained the names Bouncy Slater and Rusty Lykaon written in Japanese. The odds were 1.64 for the former and 2.39 for the latter.

"...Huh? Don't the odds usually change depending on who the people are betting on and by how much?" Asuna wondered suspiciously. That was true, but there was a special trick to this odds table.

"Just watch the numbers," I whispered as the black numerals on the parchment began to move like living animals. The two numbers changed to 1.62 and 2.40.

"Oh! They changed."

"…Get it? I bet if Kizmel saw this, she'd call it some '*strange human charm*.'"

The instant I mentioned the dark elf knight's name, Asuna's eyelids lowered with concern. It didn't last long, however.

"I see; so the numerical odds automatically update on the sheet," she said. "Meaning…there are more people who are betting on Bouncy Slater to win the first match?"

"Not necessarily. Odds are determined solely on the amount of money wagered, so it could just be a few big spenders who tilt the odds in that contestant's favor."

"I see…Anyway, I assume that the lykaon has to be a doglike monster, but what would a Bouncy Slater be?" she asked.

Argo answered first. "A slater is another name for a pill bug. One that bounces, in this case."

"Pill bug…" Asuna repeated, making a sour face.

"Which one is your client suspicious of, Argo?" I asked. "The pill bug or the lykaon?"

"The lykaon."

"…Meaning your client wants you to figure out what the trick is?"

"Correct," the info dealer said.

Just then, there was the loud *crash!* of a gong behind us, followed by an energetic announcement.

"Ladiiiies and gentlemeeeeen! *Wel*come to the crown jewel of the Volupta Grand Casino, the Battle Arenaaaa!"

I turned around and spotted a booth on the next level above the floor with the cage, where an NPC in a white shirt and red bow tie was standing in a spotlight. It was a primitive spotlight using mirrors and large lanterns, of course, not an electric one. But whether it was actually working on some logical system or just the "magic" of the virtual world, it was plenty bright.

When the crowd's applause died down, the NPC continued

speaking, his voice loud enough for everyone in the arena to hear him, despite the lack of a microphone.

"The first match of our night schedule will be starting shortly! Ticket sales are ending in just five minutes, so get those wagers in now, while you have the chance!"

A number of guests—NPCs, of course—rushed toward the ticket counter. The ALS and DKB did not move from the buffet tables because they had already bought theirs.

"I wonder if they actually bet all one thousand chips they won during the day…" I murmured skeptically.

Argo shrugged. "Probably did, yeah? If they're serious about turnin' a thousand into a hundred grand, they gotta bet everything they have on all five matches comin' up."

"Umm…"

I glanced down at the odds table again. The odds on the first match had shifted again, to 1.61 and 2.41. The subsequent matches also had payouts that hovered around two or three at the highest, but if you bet everything you had and won all five times, it would indeed be possible to reach a hundred thousand chips, starting from a thousand.

That was the trap, however. I'd won the first four bets in a similar situation during the beta and was just one match away from claiming the top prize at the casino, when…

I sighed, banishing that memory, then smirked at Argo. "Now that we know there's cheating going on, we should've bet everything on the lykaon."

"Better not! If you buy a monster battle ticket while the quest is active, you fail it," she said, shaking her head rapidly. The info dealer fixed the two of us with a dead serious look. "And I don't think this is the kind of quest where you get a do-over. Still, I'm not positive I can spot the tell on my own. Kii-boy, A-chan, I'll need yer help."

"You bet!" said Asuna brightly. I added a clumsy "Uh, y-yeah."

Within moments, the gong crashed again, and the lights in the hall dimmed.

The artificial spotlight hit the golden cage this time. Everyone in the room focused silently on the stage.

The rectangular cage was quite large, twelve feet across on the short side and thirty on the long side. Three sides of the cage were bars, while the far side was the stone wall of the room. Metal bars blocked the roof of the cage, too, and there was a partition on the inside that separated it into two parts. In the beta, the monsters simply popped into existence on either side of the cage, which struck me as lazy programming. This, too, appeared to be another area where the official release had been polished up.

Rumbling heavily, the stone wall receded in two places that subsequently began to rise upward. The NPC with the bow tie announced, "And now! Starting with the first match of the Battle Arena's night schedule! Our first combatant...a killer insect clad in steel armor! The Bouncy Slaterrrr!"

Just as Argo had described, a pill bug came plodding out of the left doorway—only it was nearly three feet long. Its tough-looking shell was bluish-black and shining.

I'd fought these enemies a few times in the beta. If you tried to slash their shells and let your strength do the work, it would only succeed at wearing down your weapon.

"And in opposition...the red reaper whose jaw can crush iron! The Rusty Lykaooon!"

A deep growl emerged from the right doorway. Out of the darkness proceeded a dog-type monster with a dark-red pelt and black spots. Lykaons were squatter than wolves, with shorter snouts, but they were hardier and had very powerful jaws. Even without the length of the tail, it was notably larger than the pill bug.

Colored cursors appeared above both monsters. They were NPC yellow rather than a shade of red, perhaps to hide the system that displayed an enemy's relative difficulty based on the tint of its color.

I focused on the lykaon. According to the person who gave Argo the quest, it was engaging in some form of foul play.

Both pill bug and lykaon were monsters that appeared in the latter half of the seventh floor. Between them, it was the pill bug that had been more trouble in the beta. The lykaons weren't easy by any means, but the danger mainly came from the fact that they appeared in packs of two or three. As long as you could isolate one and deal with it individually, they were a good source of experience. The NPC announcer claimed it could "crush iron" with its jaw, but that was a bit of exaggeration.

As a matter of fact, the odds were higher for the lykaon, meaning that the guests in the hall had put down more money overall on the pill bug. Therefore, if you placed a big counterbid on the lykaon and had some means of cheating so it would win, you stood to make major cash. The real question was how you could help the lykaon win the monster battle while all these people were watching…

"It doesn't seem particularly noteworthy, visually speaking…I was expecting to see metal dentures or claws attached…"

"Don't you think people would notice that? This isn't Battle Bots," Asuna said archly. "I was thinking that they might have fed it some kind of stimulant, but I've never seen this monster before, so I wouldn't be able to tell the difference. Can you, Kirito?"

"Hmm…It doesn't seem like it's especially agitated or anything. And wouldn't a drug like that leave an icon over its HP bar? Whether it's supposed to be a buff or a debuff."

"Ah, good point," Asuna murmured.

The bow tie announcer called out, "Will the killer steel insect crush its prey?! Or will the red reaper crack that shell with its jaw?! Let the first match…begiiiin!"

Bwaaash! The gong crashed again, and the fence that separated the two halves of the cage lowered. The pill bug's elongated abdominal eyes flashed, as did the red irises of the lykaon.

"Help me out here, you two," Argo whispered as the monsters roared and the crowd cheered.

"*Shaaaa!*" the pill bug hissed.

"*Grrooo!*" the lykaon roared. They charged together, the pill bug opening its jaw and scuttling forward on seven pairs of legs while the lykaon leaped to the right on its third step in an attempt to circle around the enemy.

The pill bug could change directions, but much more slowly. The lykaon got behind it on a diagonal and pressed the attack at once, biting one of the insect's legs.

"*Grrr!*" It locked its legs and shook its head violently, snapping the leg off at the base and spilling out bright-red damage effects.

"*Shhhoo!*" the pill bug hissed, something that could not be identified as either rage or a scream. Its HP gauge dropped about 7 percent. Cheers and howls filled the arena.

Belatedly, I wondered which one Lind's and Kibaou's groups had bet on. The answer might have been clear from their reactions, but I couldn't take my eyes off that HP bar.

The lykaon won the first attack, but that didn't seem to be the effect of cheating. The lykaon was clearly far superior in mobility, so if the pill bug rushed straight for it, of course it was going to circle around the back.

The beast attacked again and pulled out a second leg, increasing the damage to 15 percent. The NPC announcer wailed, "The red reaper scores consecutive attacks! I guess that bug's just a bug!"

The lykaon reacted as though it understood those words, taking distance and growling, "*Grrrl...*"

The severed leg in its jaw turned into blue particles that dispersed in the air. There were still twelve legs left. If it removed all of them, the pill bug wouldn't be able to walk—assuming it was even still alive. If the same thing kept repeating, that would be the result, but I knew from the trouble they caused me in the beta that this pill bug could do more than slowly rotate.

"*Shuuu...*" the pill bug growled, and it suddenly rolled itself up.

Its head, feelers, and legs all vanished inside the shining black carapace. The lykaon glared warily at the new shape of its enemy, a black ball sixteen inches across. Four or five seconds of silence passed, and someone in the audience lost patience and shouted, "Attack it, pup!"

Right on cue, there was movement—but it was the pill bug. However, instead of returning to its usual form, it flattened its rounded form, then shot up into the air with an explosive *bam!*

The pill bug launched itself upward like a rocket, first colliding with the ceiling of the cage, then reflecting downward with a shower of sparks. Like a game of three-dimensional pinball, it bounced off the cage wall, the floor, then the wall again, and slammed into the lykaon's side.

"Gyarp!" The lykaon yelped in pain as it was hurled into the side of the cage. It got to its feet immediately after falling to the ground, but that single blow took out nearly 30 percent of its health.

That high-speed bounce attack was the pill bug's one big means of offense, and it was a doozy. It was also the reason for the name Bouncy Slater. On a flat, open plain, it was easy enough to avoid a direct charge, but in the forest, it could bounce off trees, making it a two-dimensional attacker rather than one. Even worse, with the floor and ceiling in a dungeon, it became a three-dimensional attacker. I got beaten the hell up from all directions before I mastered the trick to avoiding them.

"And that's the slater's killer attack technique! Is the deadly lykaon helpless to counteract this one?!" asked the announcer. His voice was drowned out by a deluge of cheers.

The pill bug flattened its body again. The lykaon sank back, preparing to avoid the attack.

Bam! The pill bug shot off the ground again, this time reflecting off the stone wall behind it to attack its opponent from the side. The lykaon jumped high to avoid the first angle, but the pill bug merely bounced from the cage to the floor and back upward toward the still-aloft lykaon.

The wolflike creature was blasted against the ceiling and fell to the ground. Its HP was in the yellow zone, under 40 percent.

"......Uh, are you sure this thing is cheating?" I muttered reflexively. Neither Argo nor Asuna replied. Like me, they hadn't spotted anything yet.

Cheers of support arose for the hobbled lykaon, but not many. The majority of the onlookers had bet on the pill bug, it seemed.

One more solid bouncing attack would probably kill the lykaon. And given the small dimensions of the cage and the many surfaces it offered to bounce off, it seemed impossible to avoid such a three-dimensional, high-speed attack.

For the third time, the pill bug squashed itself against the ground.

The black orb shot upward at an angle. *Wha-wha-wham!* It bounced back and forth from the ceiling to the floor, approaching the wounded lykaon. The battle was over, it seemed to me.

"Graaaooooo!!"

But then the lykaon howled ferociously and leaped straight for the pill bug. A simple body blow couldn't possibly crack that tough shell; it could shatter a sword. The beast was going to get smashed and die for sure...

Until suddenly, the lykaon began to rapidly rotate around the median line of its body. It opened its jaw wide and spun at a rate that defied the laws of physics. The lykaon rushed forward like a red drill and slammed into the cannonball pill bug in midair.

An earsplitting metallic crash ripped through the air, and a huge spray of sparks issued from the point where they met. Both creatures writhed and struggled aloft, until one HP bar began to drop very rapidly. They were so close together that it was difficult to identify which one it was.

Even I found myself holding my breath, and I didn't have any money on the match.

Craaash! A huge amount of blue shards burst outward.

The furry red lykaon flew through the cloud and landed on the other side of the cage.

Several seconds of silence was broken by the frantic smashing of the gong. Angry roars, jeers, and cheers exploded from the audience, rattling the arena with their ferocity.

"Ohhhh myyyy goodness! What a *huuuuge* comeback! The winner is the red reaper, Rustyyy Lykaoooon!" screamed the bow tie.

It was loud enough that I barely heard Argo mutter, "Hang on; do Rusty Lykaons have a special attack like that…?"

"I never saw it during the beta," I told her, "but plenty of monsters have received new attack patterns since then. Maybe this is one of them."

"In that case, it's a good thing we saw it here. Even *you'd* have trouble perfectly deflecting an attack like that on your first try, Master Black."

I was tempted to be outraged, but she was right, of course. A canine-type monster performing a high-speed spinning attack was simply beyond the bounds of imagination. Even if I managed to defend, the force of it would snap my sword in two.

The bettors couldn't have anticipated it, either. The more unsavory NPCs in the standing area swore loudly and furiously, while exclamations of disappointment could be heard from the seats behind us.

The gong crashed again, and the gateway in the stone wall opened once more, but only on the right side this time. The victorious lykaon vanished into the darkness, limping slightly, as the bow tie announcer declared, "That's the end of our first match! A round of applause for our winner, Rusty Lykaon!"

The audience clapped for the winner, but given that more of them had bet on the loser, there wasn't much enthusiasm behind it. That didn't bother the announcer, who continued energetically, "Thank you! Our second match will begin in ten minutes, at nine twenty! There are still tickets available for purchase, so if you want to grow your winnings or make up what you lost, step right up the counter, folks!"

The spotlight on the announcer's stand faded, and the room got a bit brighter. In the relaxed atmosphere that followed, the people milling around trickled toward the exit or the buffet bars.

That made me wonder how the results affected our fellow players. I stared at the table where the DKB had been seated. Lind, Shivata, and Hafner were raising narrow fluted glasses. Apparently they'd bet on the lykaon and multiplied their winnings by 2.41.

Then I turned to look at the ALS on the other side of the room. I very nearly murmured "*No way*" when I saw them. Kibaou's group was raising mugs of ale and having a toast with huge smiles on every face. They certainly didn't seem to be drinking to mourn a loss.

I turned to the two girls, who were still examining the combat cage, and said, "Seems like Lin-Kiba both won."

"Eugh, no way," muttered Argo. Great minds think alike. "I figured that one of the two woulda lost it all there. That means they both got two thousand four hundred chips...What now? What if they both make a hundred thousand, and they both get that big shiny sword? Assuming there's two of 'em to share."

"Uh, w-we won't do a thing. If it speeds up our pace through the game, that's a good thing..."

I gave the honor student response. But of course, I couldn't deny that I was just the teensiest bit—maybe half a teaspoon— jealous of the idea. I might have been a prisoner of *SAO*, but I was also undeniably an online gamer.

Diavel the knight, the man who laid the foundation for today's frontline group, went through Argo in a scheme to buy my Anneal Blade from me and made a reckless charge against the boss of the first floor in an attempt to win the Last Attack bonus. Now that other players had caught up to us in terms of level and gear, I understood his motivations. Or maybe that was presumptuous of me to say. After all, Diavel had wanted strength in order to save the prisoners of Aincrad, while at the end of the day, I only had interest in my own power.

I was broken out of this rare instance of self-reflection by Asuna, who turned away from the cage to ask, "So the special attack the lykaon used *wasn't* cheating?"

To my surprise, she hadn't employed her usual psychic ability to sense my negative thoughts. "Y-yeah," I said quickly. "If that was cheating, then the pill bug's bouncing attack would be, too."

"True…Sorry, Argo, I'm afraid I don't have any idea what sort of cheating that lykaon may have been doing," Asuna said.

Argo shook her head. "Nah, you don't need to apologize. I didn't have a clue, either…You notice anything, Kii-boy?"

With the attention on me, all I could do was raise my palms. "No idea. When the lykaon got hit by the pill bug's reflecting attack and smashed into the cage, I thought it was dead…Has the quest log been updated at all?"

"Let's see…" Argo leaned over, opened her window, then looked up and shook her head again. "Nope, no difference. It still says FIGURE OUT THE IMPROPER ACTIONS USED ON THE LYKAON IN THE FIRST MATCH OF THE BATTLE ARENA'S NIGHT SCHEDULE."

"And no hints, huh? We haven't failed the quest yet, either…"

I glanced at the spot where the lykaon struck the golden cage. It couldn't have been pure gold, I assumed. Despite the impact, the vertical bars weren't bent or dented in the least. I guessed they had to be just as indestructible as the building itself. Otherwise, there was the chance that a larger and more powerful monster might smash through and endanger the audience.

Even if such an event happened, we were within the anti-criminal-code zone, so players couldn't lose HP. But what about the NPCs? And how were they bringing these monsters into town to have them fight anyway…?

There was no end to the questions I could come up with. My mind worked relentlessly as my eyes fixed on the golden cage.

"……Hmm?"

I noticed something. My brows lowered.

A number of the shining, polished golden bars were stained with a reddish something. Right at the spot where the lykaon hit the cage.

Well, if you hit a hard surface with that much force, some blood is to be expected, I thought. But there was no "bloodshed" in *SAO* at all. I'd never even seen bloodstains left behind after any battles in the game. There was the bloody handprint left on the golden cube from the "Curse of Stachion" quest, where Cylon had beaten his master Pithagrus to death, but that was just part of the quest story…

"…Oh."

I murmured again and looked down at myself. I'd removed my armor so I was only wearing a black shirt and pants—and my shortsword. There was nothing in my pockets.

"Do either of you have a handkerchief or something else you don't mind discarding? Preferably a white one," I asked Asuna and Argo, who were reading the latter's quest log on party-visible mode. Argo merely rolled her eyes, but Asuna said exasperatedly, "You should have one of your own, Kirito."

"W-well, I normally keep one in my belt pouch…but it's not white."

"Will this do?" she said, pulling a perfectly white handkerchief from the large front pocket of her dress.

"I probably won't be able to give it back. Is that all right?"

"It's fine. I can just make more with the Tailoring skill."

I didn't even wait for the end of the sentence before I snatched it away and rushed six feet to the left. With a quick glance around to make sure that neither Kibaou, Lind, nor any NPCs were watching, I reached up with the handkerchief and rubbed firmly at the red stain on the bars of the cage.

Once I'd gotten enough, I stepped away and stared at the cloth. The red color looked too vivid to be dried blood to me…but I couldn't be absolutely positive, because this was a virtual world and all.

"Is that the lykaon's blood, Kii-boy?"

"If you wanted to rub the cage, you could have asked for a rag."

Undeterred by the skeptical comments from the women, I lifted the red stain to my nose and sniffed. There was none of the particular iron stink of blood. Instead, it had a very faintly sweet, perhaps floral scent. I suspected it was not the actual smell of the lykaon's blood, but rather, it was…

"This isn't blood," I murmured, drawing looks from Argo and Asuna.

"If it ain't blood, then what is it?"

"Probably some kind of dye…"

"Dye? Why would it be—?"

Argo paused, then looked to the left—not behind me but to a message on the left side of her line of sight.

"…Quest log just got updated."

"Huh? What does it say?" asked Asuna, leaning forward. Argo opened her quest window again and pointed. I sidled around and looked over Asuna's shoulder.

The updated quest log said: YOU HAVE DISCOVERED THE ILLE-GITIMATE TACTIC USED ON THE LYKAON. REPORT BACK TO THE QUESTGIVER. Argo grinned, having figured out the trick, and held out her fist. I gave her knuckles, but Asuna still looked confused.

"So the dye was evidence of cheating? Why would that…… Oh!"

She figured it out, too, before I needed to explain it to her. But we didn't want to talk about it out loud and be overheard. I held a shushing finger to my lips and whispered to Argo, "Is the quest-giver nearby?"

"In the hotel on the third floor."

"Really? The VIP area? Do you have a pass?"

"The questgiver gave me a one-day pass kinda thing. Don't worry, I can get friends through…I think."

That last comment left me a little worried, but we were already along for the ride. It was a shame I wouldn't get to watch the sec-ond match, but we weren't placing bets anyway.

"Okay, let's go."

"Sure thing. Just be on yer best behavior, Kii-boy," she said, *only* to me, and then turned to leave. As we rushed after her, I glanced over and saw Asuna biting her lips, trying desperately not to laugh.

6

TRYING TO AVOID THE ATTENTION OF THE ALS AND DKB, we slipped through the crowd and out of the arena, where we felt free to exhale with relief. Perhaps they had noticed us a while ago but were too busy to bother caring about us. I'd looked at the odds for the second match, which were currently 2.07 and 2.75. If they bet everything on the higher odds and won again, they'd have at least six thousand six hundred chips.

But why had they been so sure that betting on the lykaon, which had higher odds—meaning less chance of winning—would be successful? Were they just hoping for the bigger payout, or did they have some kind of tip-off about its real chance of winning? I couldn't help but wonder.

I picked up speed to reach Argo on the stairs back to the first-floor hall and muttered under my breath, "Do you think it's possible that Lin-Kiba took the same quest you did?"

"Huh? Oh…because they both bet on the Rusty Lykaon," said the info dealer, instantly catching on to my logic. She considered it and said, "Hmm, I can't rule it out entirely, but I doubt it. This quest wasn't in the beta, and it was real hard to find the starting point…I have a hard time imagining that either ALS or DKB found it the moment they came to Volupta."

She took a breath, then continued, "For one thing, the only match the quest tells ya there's cheatin' involved was the one we just saw. Doesn't explain how they won all the bets in the day-time, does it?"

"Oh...Ah, right..."

That explanation made sense, but it didn't clear up *why* the ALS and DKB made so many chips. The monsters in the arena were appearing for the first time in the game, so they couldn't bet based on experience and knowledge of their abilities. Were Lind and Kibaou just that lucky? If they actually won ten all-or-nothing bets in a row and acquired the Sword of Volupta, I was going to have to take a long, hard look at my game strategy.

My mood was souring, and I had to take a deep breath to re-center myself. I felt like I'd been antsy ever since setting foot in this town. Maybe I still had some lingering enthusiasm for gambling after getting burned in the beta, but I wasn't a solo player without any obligation to anyone else anymore. I was the one who invited Asuna to play with me on the first floor. I had a responsibility to be her partner until she was ready for the next stage.

With these thoughts in mind, I glanced to my right, where the fencer in question was staring at the red carpet, deep in thought. Unfortunately, my interpersonal communication skill was at too low of a level for me to guess what she was thinking. She would probably tell me if I asked, but even that question was a big hurdle for an eighth-grade boy.

We finished the climb up the stairs to the ground floor hall and rounded the goddess statue on the way to the other end, where the staircase to the second floor waited, guarded by an NPC dressed in black—and a red-velvet rope.

Sandals flapping, Argo strode right up to the tough-looking bouncer, who was probably just as dangerous as the town guard NPCs, and held up a gray metal tag she'd produced at some point.

"Can my two companions and I get through?" she asked. The man silently detached the rope from one of the poles and pulled it back, giving a sullen bow. Argo walked right past him, and Asuna and I followed.

We continued up more stairs, hearing the rope clicking back into place behind us. On the second floor, Argo ignored the VIP high-roller game room and crossed the red carpet to the next set of stairs.

The third-floor hall was octagonal, like the others, but its lights were low, and the carpet was black, seeming to absorb everything it touched. There was supposedly a fourth floor, but I saw no staircase. In the center of the room was a statue that looked like a priest with the head of a fish.

"...Why a fish?" I asked, looking up at the statue.

Asuna tilted her head. "I've heard the headgear that Catholic bishops wear is supposed to be in the shape of a fish head...but this doesn't seem to be related."

"It's a creepy-looking face."

"And not exactly like the ichthyoids from the fourth floor."

While we talked, Argo stepped to a stately counter in the back of the hall, showing her metal tag to the NPC there. Then she turned back and waved her hand to beckon us closer.

We hurried forward, at which point Argo started walking down a hallway leading farther into the building. The stringed instrument music, which was supposedly being performed on the second floor, was completely out of earshot now. The silence in the hallway was painfully loud. At the end, we turned left, then right, and walked a ways farther before stopping at a door.

"Room seventeen...This is the place," Argo murmured, then rapped sharply on the dark, heavy door twice.

A few moments later, a faint voice from inside said, "Who is it?"

"Argo. And my companions...er, my assistants."

After another pause, there was the dainty click of a lock turning. The door pushed open slowly, revealing an interior that was even darker than the hallway.

It made me wonder if we should go back to equipping our gear, or at least our swords—but I thought better of it when I noticed that Argo wasn't concerned in the least as she walked inside. Technically, I still had my shortsword at my side, so if anything happened, I could at least make do for Asuna until she could put on her full battle equipment.

The room through the door was so extravagant that it immediately made the platinum suite at the Ambermoon Inn pale in comparison. The only light came from a few lamps, but there was plenty of moonlight streaming through a massive window on the south end of the room. In front of it was a sofa that could easily seat five people at once.

Only one person was sitting on it now.

I could just make out the silhouette, but it was quite small. Focusing on it produced a yellow NPC cursor. The name beneath the HP gauge was Nirrnir, but I wasn't quite sure how to pronounce it. Above her head was a floating ? symbol, the sign of a quest in progress.

Nurnur...? Neenir...? Near-nire? I tried sounding out various permutations in my head but was interrupted by a woman's voice to my left.

"I will take what is on your waist."

"*Fwee?!*" I squealed, jumping away in pure reaction and bumping into Asuna on my right.

"Hey! Watch out," she grumbled, but she supported my weight anyway. I whispered a quick apology, then looked into the darkness to the left.

Standing next to the door was a maid in a black dress and white apron...or so I thought at first. She was actually wearing a dark, gleaming breastplate, and her skirt was adorned with lines of arrowhead-shaped metal plates. On top of that, she wore gloves and boots, as well as a rapier on her left hip—except it was a purely thrusting weapon, with no blade whatsoever. An estoc, then.

In terms of anime and Japanese games, warrior maids were practically a tradition at this point, but I couldn't remember seeing anyone like this in Aincrad before. The color cursor was yellow, like the person on the couch. Her name was Kio, which seemed easy enough to say. *Kee-oh.*

I was staring at her absentmindedly when the maid, who had crisply parted hair and sharp eyes, glared at me and demanded, "Your sword."

"Oh…! H-here."

I was worried about losing my weapon, but I did have the martial arts skill, too, I told myself, removing the shortsword's sheath from my belt. The maid quickly took it away from me, then pulled it out halfway to examine the blade.

"…Plain steel."

I was tempted to quip something like "Sorry it's not pure orichalcum" but thought better of it, because I knew she wouldn't get it. The maid then placed the shortsword on a nearby rack and stepped back.

"Please do not give offense to Lady Nirrnir," she said. She pronounced the name something like *Neer-nur*. I was wise enough not say out loud what an odd and interesting name I thought it was.

With the permission of Kio the warrior maid, Argo walked farther into the room. Asuna and I followed her.

We crossed the absurdly deep carpet toward the regal sofa, until we could finally see this Lady Nirrnir. Now it made sense why her figure seemed so small as it leaned against the many cushions—she couldn't have been more than twelve years old.

She wore a black dress made of a many-layered but rather transparent material—tulle or organdy or something like that. Her skin was so pale, and her flowing blond hair was so fine and shining that, for a moment, I thought she was just a doll.

Her head moved, revealing features that were beautiful, young, and mysterious in the moonlight. Red lips parted to issue a soft, high-pitched voice with just a hint of a lisp.

"Welcome back, Argo. Did you find your assistants?"

"Yeah, I've known them for a little while now. Say hello to Miss Nirr," said Argo, who seemed no different from her usual self, which didn't make it any easier to know how to act here. Asuna stepped forward and greeted her in a way I'd only ever seen in movies. She pinched the hem of her dress, pulled her right leg back, and bent her left knee.

"It's an honor to meet you, Miss Nirrnir. My name is Asuna."

She straightened up and took a step back. Next was my turn, but I had no skirt in order to mimic Asuna. My brain was overheating, trying desperately to remember what noblemen in foreign movies did. Like Asuna, I pulled my right leg back and crossed it with my left leg, then placed my right hand below my chest and extended my left hand straight to the side, then bowed.

"N-nice to meet you. I'm Kirito."

I had no idea if this was right, but the girl nodded generously and asked, "Asuna and Kirito...Is this correct?" That was a pronunciation check, something that nearly every AI-run NPC asked. Her intonation was perfect, so we said yes.

"I see. Good evening. Will you sit?"

She pointed not at an empty spot on the enormous sofa but at a three-person sofa facing her. I sat down, then Argo and Asuna, and Kio promptly began setting out teacups on the marble table. When did she prepare that? When she was done, she slid out of sight, holding the tray, to wait at a location equidistant to the sofas. She was close enough that if I tried to do anything funny to her master, she could skewer me with that estoc.

I had no intention of testing out that hypothesis, of course. I thanked her for the tea and took a sip. It was straight tea, with no sugar or milk, but there was a muscat grape scent to it—and just the tiniest hint of sweetness. To my right, Asuna exclaimed that it was delicious, so that told me it was very fine tea, indeed.

Once we'd placed our cups down, Nirrnir straightened up about halfway from her slumped position and said, "Since you've come back, does that mean you've figured out the cheat involving that doggy, Argo?"

"I'm pretty sure. Go ahead and explain what you found, Kii-boy."

This caught me by surprise. "Whaaat?!" I protested, but I knew I couldn't refuse. Instead, I pulled the carefully folded handkerchief out of my pants pocket. I rose to my feet, intending to lean forward and hand Nirrnir the handkerchief, when Kio approached from the right and held out her hand.

"…Ah. Thanks."

I placed the handkerchief in her palm. Kio opened it up and looked at the red stain in the middle, frowning. She then walked around the back of the ornate couch, knelt at the right side of her master, and held out the cloth.

Nirrnir plucked it out of her hand, looking suspicious.

"…What does this mean, Kirito?" she asked.

"That stain was left behind when the Rusty Lykaon, the winner of the match, hit the side of the cage."

"So this is…*not* the dog's blood? It doesn't smell like blood," said Nirrnir conclusively, despite the fact that she had not leaned down to sniff it.

I nodded. "Yes. I believe it's a dye taken from some kind of plant."

"A dye…?"

Nirrnir's big, doll-like eyes narrowed. I'd thought her irises were black, but in the angle of the moonlight, I saw they were a deep red.

"Meaning the dog's fur was dyed this color?"

"That's right," I agreed, and then I explained the trick in as clear a voice as possible: "Rusty Lykaons appear on the western side of this floor, in the Field of Bones. But there's no reason to dye one the same color they already are…meaning that the pill bug—er, the Bouncy Slater—was not actually fighting a Rusty Lykaon but a more advanced species with a different colored pelt."

"……"

Nirrnir did not speak after my explanation was over. I started to worry that I might have gotten something wrong, but then the girl moved, returning the handkerchief to Kio. Her left hand remained outstretched, waiting for something.

Kio quickly stashed the evidence handkerchief into her apron pocket, then picked up a wine bottle from a nearby side table. She poured about two fingers of dark liquid into a glass.

Nirrnir allowed her to place the glass into her waiting hand, then drained its contents in one go, which I assumed was red wine. *That kid's drinking alcohol! You're gonna be in trouble!* I thought, but then I realized Aincrad probably didn't have any laws against underage drinking.

To my surprise, Nirrnir lifted the empty glass, preparing to smash it against the ground. But she composed herself, slowly lowered her hand, and gave the glass to Kio. She exhaled slowly, paused, then looked up at us.

Her fine brows were sharply tilted, and suddenly there was no longer any hint of youth in her beauty. She couldn't have been more than a year apart from Myia, the girl from the sixth floor, but the force of her presence was unlike any girl I'd ever met.

"...The old Korloy bastard's really done it now."

Her voice was hot with the flames of anger, but the presence of an unfamiliar name caused me to ask, "Who's Korloy?"

"...Explain for them, Kio," she proclaimed, waving her hand. Kio set the wine glass down on the table, then returned to her usual position and looked down at me.

"Are you aware that the Volupta Grand Casino is run by the Nachtoy family, of which Lady Nirrnir is the matriarch, and also the Korloys, who are relatives?"

I'd never heard either name, not even in the beta. I glanced to the right and saw Argo and Asuna shaking their heads. To Kio I said, "I apologize, I—I did not know that."

"...That is no surprise, if you are an adventurer newly arrived to this town. The Nachtoys and Korloys are both descendants of the hero Falhari. You must know the name Falhari, surely."

It sounded familiar, but I couldn't place it. Fortunately, I didn't need to overturn my jumbled memories, because Asuna bailed me out.

"That's the person who vanquished Zariegha the water dragon and founded Volupta."

"Correct. Falhari took for his wife the girl who was to be given to Zariegha as a sacrifice, and they had twin sons. But the boys were terrible enemies, and when they grew up, they battled over the right to be Falhari's heir. In his old age, Falhari forbid his sons from taking up swords against one another. Instead, he instructed them to tame monsters to do their fighting. By his decree, whoever won three out of five matches would be the next ruler of Volupta."

"Uh-huh…"

That might have been a more peaceful resolution than twin brothers fighting to the death, but it had to suck for the monsters, I thought.

Nirrnir practically read my mind. "You adventurers have killed countless monsters, too, of course."

"R-right. You're correct," I replied feebly. Nirrnir snorted softly, then waved at Kio to continue.

"…After Falhari the Founder passed on, the twins followed his decree and enacted a five-match series of battles using tamed monsters."

"Wait, h-hang on," I said, interrupting just as she had started her explanation. Kio gave me a very cross look. I hunched my shoulders guiltily and asked, "You say tamed as though it's that easy…Is it even possible?"

"Not for ordinary people like you or me," the maid claimed. Then she added proudly, "But Falhari the hero knew the secret art of controlling monsters. The twins inherited that power from him and used it to tame them."

"Secret art…" I repeated, in blank shock. As quietly as possible, I murmured into Argo's ear, "*SAO* doesn't have a monster-taming skill, right?"

"It's not in the list of skills you can choose. If it exists, it must be an Extra Skill…"

"Oh man," I muttered, swallowing.

The two Extra Skills in my skill slots, martial arts and Meditation, both required clearing a kind of trial quest from an NPC. Was this quest one of those, too? If we finished it, could we gain the Taming skill that people believed didn't exist in *SAO*…?

"May I continue?" Kio asked archly.

I snapped back to attention. "Ah! Y-yes, please do."

"After the Founder, Falhari, passed on, the twins followed his decree and enacted a five-match series of battles using tamed monsters," Kio said, repeating the exact same words she'd said before I interrupted. "But neither of them had much confidence in the monsters he'd prepared. So just to see if they were ready to conduct the proper duel, they agreed to an informal test beforehand. They built a wooden fence around an empty space in front of their mansion, with two exits. The plan was to insert the monsters through the exit, so they would fight inside the fence. The test ended up being conducted with a large crowd of curious villagers watching. The monsters simply leaped over the fence or were so strong they destroyed it in their battling. It caused quite a stir."

Well, no wonder, with just a wooden fence, I thought. But that was not the end of Kio's story.

"However, there were no deaths or injuries among the townspeople, and the crowd seemed to really enjoy the exhibition. At the time, Volupta was just a small village built on fishing and farming, and there wasn't much entertainment in Lectio to the east or Pramio to the west. The next week, they held a second test with reinforced fences, and it brought crowds not just from Volupta but Lectio and Pramio as well. They set up stands, placed bets, and gave the event a festival atmosphere."

"...I think I can see where this is goin'," whispered Argo. I did, too. Kio was no longer glaring at us, but she was lost deep in her story of the past, making gestures with her hands to punctuate the descriptions.

"The twins noticed this reaction and had an idea. What if, rather than rushing into their best-of-five match to determine the answer, they repeated these test matches over and over? They could draw guests to Volupta each week, eager to spend their money. That hunch was proven correct, and when they officially turned the test battles into a coliseum battle, the visitors poured in from the other two towns. The competition for the inheritance went to the wayside, as the twins took control of the betting themselves, adding warm-up entertainment and other wagering games. Soon they had renovated their family mansion, until it became the Volupta Grand Casino you see today. The twins grew old and passed away, leaving the operation in their children's hands, then grandchildren, until the last will of Falhari the Founder became no more than a story..."

Kio trailed off there, and Nirrnir added:

"As you saw in the basement, the test fights no longer have any connection to their original purpose. They are held day and night here."

"......"

Based on the clipped, frank tone of the young lady's voice, it was impossible to tell what she thought about the decree of the founder, which was now nothing more than an empty husk. I didn't even know how many generations away from Falhari the hero she was.

According to the dark elf legends Kizmel taught us, Aincrad the floating castle had been carved out of the earth below in the distant past, with all its various towns and villages, and banished to the distant sky, where no magic could reach it. It wasn't clear how long ago the "distant past" was supposed to be, but it had to be way more than a century or two.

Kizmel had also said, *Only Her Royal Majesty possesses all the legends surrounding the Great Separation and the six sacred keys. All that we are told is that this floating castle was created long in the past.* But if we knew how many years ago Falhari the hero lived, we could at least establish a minimum range for the "distant past."

I summoned my courage to ask Nirrnir about that topic. But a split second before I could speak, Asuna said, "If the twins inherited the hero Falhari's power, does that mean that, as a part of that bloodline, you are able to tame monsters, too, Miss Nirrnir?"

"That's right," she replied.

Kio added, "To be precise, it is Lady Nirrnir, the head of the Nachtoy family, and one other...the head of the Korloy family, Bardun. Only they can use the power of 'employment.'"

"Meaning that half the monsters fighting in the Battle Arena downstairs every day...were tamed personally by you, my lady?"

"Right," she said, just as briefly. Although, perhaps because Asuna was 50 percent more polite than me, she also added, "However, I do not trudge through forests and mountains and caves. I merely tame creatures that are captured and brought to me. I *want* to go searching for them. But Kio and the guards will not allow me."

"Of course not!" Kio interjected. "Your life is in danger from the Korloys, Lady Nirrnir. To venture into the wild would be begging them to attack you."

"At this point, I would appreciate a good honest attack over all these poisons and tricks."

I couldn't help but comment on this rather grisly conversation. "Um, your life is in danger...? I thought the Nachtoys and Korloys run the Grand Casino together. If the person who's supplying half the monsters for the arena disappears, won't that be a bad thing for the Korloys' business, too?"

"Unfortunately, Bardun Korloy has grown too senile to understand obvious logic like yours. Old age is a terrible curse," Nirrnir said, a rather strange thing for a child to have an opinion about, and she sank back into the cushions. She lifted her crossed legs up into the air, waving gently, and said in a voice not much more than a whisper, "In the past...Bardun cared for me. But as the end of his life grew closer, he became obsessed with prolonging it. Now Bardun is obsessed with gathering all the gold he can to buy scant moments of life, and he's lost sight of everything else. That is why he's sunk to these cheap tricks in the arena. The ten percent of each bet that is taken as the casino's fee goes entirely to the winner of the fight."

"Buy...life? From who?"

No healing potion you could buy at a shop, nor even the

ultra-rare healing crystals you could find on this floor, could prolong your lifespan. Hence my question, but Nirrnir just shook her head, sending her golden waves of hair swaying.

"You do not need to know that. For now...I must thank you for figuring out the trick placed on the lykaon. Kio?"

The maid bowed and walked over to us. When Argo stood up, she put a small leather sack into the Rat's hand.

"Thanks!" Argo said, taking the sack. The floating ? mark over Nirrnir's head vanished with a faint sound. The quest we were sharing had been finished. It was the end of our job, but in terms of telling a story, it was quite an unsatisfying conclusion, I thought.

At that very moment, a ! mark appeared right over the reclining girl's head, the sign of a new quest. Before she had even put the sack away, Argo promptly asked, "Do you have any other jobs, Miss Nirr?"

"Well...I suppose I do. But this one will be quite a lot of work."

"No problem. Kirito and Asuna will do the heavy lifting," Argo reassured her. Nirrnir giggled and sat up—and then turned dead serious.

"I will explain what I need. Tomorrow night, the Korloys intend to again use that Rusty Lykaon whose ruse you saw through."

"Huh? But it lost a lot of hit poi...I mean, it was injured rather badly," I pointed out.

The girl's delicate shoulders moved up and down. "I assume they will treat its wounds, of course. That lykaon has already appeared for four consecutive days."

"So it's on a four-game winning streak...But wait. Does that mean you could sense that something was wrong about the lykaon before today's match?"

"It was three days ago...I noticed during its second match," Nirrnir replied.

"In that case," I said hesitantly, "why didn't you use a stronger monster against it? The Bouncy Slater isn't exactly weak, but... you could go with a Verdian Rock Boar, or a Braising Newt, or..."

Those were names of powerful enemies from the seventh floor, plucked from my memory banks. But the girl made a sour face.

"Rock boars are too big to fit through the cage entrance, and if you fight with Braising Newts, you're going to have a fire. Besides, how are you going to set up proper odds in a match where one side has an overwhelming advantage?"

"In that case…how do you decide the matchups?"

"I have a handy list of all the monsters that are small enough to fight safely inside the cage, along with their features."

I noticed Argo twitch at the mention of that list. It was only natural that an info seller would covet that paper. *Please don't try to steal it*, I prayed as the young mistress continued her story.

"Based on their relative strength, each monster is classified as one of twelve ranks. Only monsters of the same rank can be placed in direct battle in the arena. Both the Bouncy Slater and the Rusty Lykaon are sixth-ranked monsters."

"And if I could ask…?"

"First rank is the weakest, and twelfth rank is the strongest. Meaning they used a monster that was at least seventh rank in order to take the place of a sixth-ranked Rusty Lykaon," she said, reading my mind once again. Nirrnir's deep-red eyes glinted dangerously. "No matter how the Nachtoys and Korloys may have clashed and bickered, we have *always* respected the fairness of the Grand Casino. But now Bardun has crossed the line, just for a slight increase in profit. He must be made to pay for this transgression."

"Hang on; when you said this was gonna be a lot of work, you weren't talkin' about *assassination*, were ya?" Argo asked, no need for subtlety.

The girl grimaced. "No, I would not ask that of you. If I wanted someone killed, I would do it myself," she said easily. But with those doll-like hands, she could barely swing a dagger, much less a sword. NPC stats couldn't be identified at a glance, and Myia was way too strong for a child when she fought alongside us on the previous floor, but she'd been trained by her mother, Theano.

Nirrnir was a true, pampered lady. We'd know the truth if we got her in the party and saw her level number, but that wasn't likely to ever happen.

In just two seconds, Nirrnir was back to her default expression. "I would like for you to gather the fruit of the narsos tree—and wurtz stones. If you mix equal parts squeezed juice and stones, then simmer it on low heat, it will turn into a powerful bleaching agent that strips out all dyes from a material."

"Strips out dye..." I repeated blankly, then realized what she meant. "So we'll be able to take the artificial color out of the Rusty Lykaon's fur...?"

"In the arena, right before the match. If the cheating is exposed before a hundred-plus gamblers with money on the line, even wily Bardun Korloy won't be able to wriggle out of that one."

"But...in that case, won't it cause major damage to the reputation of the casino? I imagine it might also hurt the Nachtoy family," I pointed out gingerly.

Nirrnir just sighed. "It is unavoidable. It angers me that the monsters I brought were killed by one of a different rank, but I cannot overlook cheating at my casino. We will have to issue a public apology and return the money we took from every match the lykaon appeared in."

Now I was sincerely wondering if she was actually a child. Nirrnir looked from me to Argo.

"So will you accept my request?"

"Hmmmm..."

It was very rare to see Argo being indecisive. She looked at the girl and her maid and said, "You asked me to figure out the lykaon's deception because you couldn't have someone from the Nachtoy family camping out in front of the cage, I assume. But do you really need us to gather stones and fruits? You gotta have some experienced monster hunters, and I imagine they could get what you need..."

"Of course, in terms of skill, our hunters are more than capable enough to do the job," answered Kio. "But there are two problems. First, wurtz stones can be located in the riverbed to the west of Volupta, but there are few of them to be found, and they are black, so they can only be spotted during the day. If someone from the Korloy family was to witness Nachtoy men searching for wurtz stones…"

"You'd tip 'em off that you're making the bleaching agent."

"Precisely. And the other ingredient, narsos fruit, grows in the forest in the center of the seventh floor, far from Volupta. The problem there is not the Korloys, but something else. There is a dark elf fortress in Looserock Forest."

My back straightened the moment I heard that. Asuna probably did the same.

Kio glanced at me but continued her explanation. "The Nachtoys and Korloys have long had a practice of capturing monsters in the forest while the dark elves are not watching. At this point, the dark elves attack as soon as they spot one of our hunting parties. Even our savviest hunters cannot beat the elven knights and bowmen in the forest."

Of course they couldn't. The dark elves and forest elves were always set to be many levels more powerful than the monsters that typically appeared on that floor, and here on the seventh, we might see some of their elite classes. Even I couldn't beat them in a one-on-one fight. Thankfully, as long as we had the Sigil of Lyusula, the dark elves wouldn't attack us.

Kio, as psychic as ever, gazed at the ring on my left hand and added, "Kirito, Asuna, it would seem that you have a friendship pact with the dark elves. In that case, I do not think they will attack you for simply collecting some fruits in their forest. Although I would not test what happens if you cut down living trees or break their branches."

"Uh…nope. No cutting down or breaking here."

"That is a good idea. Now, will you accept this request?"

Only Argo could answer the question. After two seconds of silence, she muttered, "Well, it wouldn't feel right to stop now," and stood up. Asuna and I hurriedly followed.

"Awright, you're on," said Argo. Instantly, the *!* mark over Nirrnir's head turned to a *?*. If it wasn't my imagination, she might have looked just a little bit relieved.

The little matriarch said, "I'm glad. What I want from you is twenty ripened narsos fruits and, oh, fifty wurtz stones. It is a three-hour trip to Looserock Forest and back, and a person can collect that many wurtz stones in five hours. When you consider the time to juice the fruits and boil the mixture, you will need to bring those materials back by one o'clock in the afternoon tomorrow for us to be ready by the time of the arena match."

"One o'clock. Got it. We'll figure it out. Guess we should get some sleep for the night, then."

"I wish I could let you stay here at the hotel, but I cannot offer you such a gift yet," Nirrnir apologized, but Argo just smirked.

"Can't ask ya to break the rules of the Grand Casino, Miss Nirr. Anyway, we'll be back here by lunchtime tomorrow."

I bowed quickly to Nirrnir and Kio, wondering if it was wise for Argo to make promises like that. But I didn't get two steps toward the door before the maid called me back.

"You forgot something, Kirito."

I turned around and saw Kio handing me the shortsword she'd taken from me—with a very exasperated look on her face. I took it quickly and resumed moving toward the door. I thought Nirrnir might have giggled a little, but that was probably just my imagination.

7

WE TOOK THE STAIRS DOWN TO THE FIRST FLOOR AND were heading out of the casino when I remembered something, so I called out to Asuna and Argo.

"Ah, hang on. Can I go and see what happened with the ALS's and DKB's bets?"

The two girls were staring coldly at me before the words were all the way out of my mouth, so I quickly shook my head to reassure them.

"No, no, not because I'm jealous. I'm just saying: What if there's some weird reason that they've been winning big?"

"Well…I guess I can't rule that out. But I don't think they've hit the final match yet," Argo pointed out. I glanced at the clock readout. It felt like we'd been talking for a long time in Nirrnir's room, but it was only ten minutes after ten PM.

If memory served, the matches of the night schedule happened at nine, nine-twenty, nine-forty, ten, and ten thirty. That meant the fourth match had probably just wrapped up. If both guilds were still on a winning streak, they would both be in an absolute frenzy right now.

"I'm only going to see!" I claimed, hurrying down the basement stairs. The moment I passed through the doors to the Battle Arena, the excitement of the gamblers washed over me.

If they hadn't lost in the second or third match, the DKB and

ALS would still be at their dining tables. I slipped through the milling NPCs in search of a spot with a clear view of the bars, when…

"Huh? Kirito?"

I twitched, coming to a panicked stop.

To my right was a woman wearing a baggy half-sleeve shirt and baggy three-quarter pants. Her orange-ish hair was cut neatly over her thick eyebrows, and below that, her eyes and nose were cute and childish. It felt like I might've seen that face somewhere before…

"…Who are you, again?" I asked awkwardly. The girl looked up at me sullenly, then pointed above her own head. Floating along with her color cursor was the name LITEN.

"Oh! Ohhh, Liten!" I shouted, right as Asuna caught up with me and slapped me on the back.

"You forgot what she looked like? That's really rude, Kirito!"

"I—I didn't forget who she was. It's just that she's not wearing her usual plate armor."

"That's another way of sayin' you forgot what she looks like," Argo helpfully pointed out.

"But I've barely ever seen her actual face!"

"Then you should be lookin' at her cursor."

"If I look at her cursor, it's going to make it obvious I don't remember her name," I argued.

Liten's pout suddenly exploded into laughter. "Ah-ha-ha-ha… You folks haven't changed a bit."

Liten was known as the plate armor girl of ALS. Not only was she one of the few women in the frontline group but she was also a crucial tank with top-class physical defense. We'd been on friendly terms with her ever since she'd helped us out during the ALS's shortcut-taking incident on the fifth floor, but as an awkward teen, I wasn't always very comfortable in her presence. That was because Liten had a partner, the track-and-field member from DKB, Shivata. I had no idea how to act around a "girl with a boyfriend"—how friendly were you allowed to be?

So I chose to keep myself about three feet away and was careful not to get too casual when speaking to her.

"Umm…So where were you going just now, Liten? The fifth match is about to start, isn't it?"

"Ah, that…" she said, glancing behind her at the buffet bar. "I got too nervous and sweaty, so I decided I'd rather not watch the fifth match in person."

"No! What a waste!" I yelled.

Asuna pushed me out of the way. "I know how you feel. I'm not a fan of this kind of weird tension, either."

"Exactly. Even the floor boss fights are better. At least there I'm *doing* something."

"Where were you going to wait for the results to come back, Liten?"

"I don't know; I was just going to wander around the first floor, I suppose…"

"Then why not come with us and have some tea?"

"Oh, that sounds lovely! But all the places around the casino are so expensive…"

"The bar counters in the first-floor casino room have normal prices."

"Let's go there, then."

It was such a quick and efficient conversation that it might as well have come out of a script. The two women started walking toward the exit. I made eye contact with Argo, then followed their lead. This was unexpected, but getting to hear the story straight from Liten would be huge.

We went up the stairs to the playroom. The bar counters were on the left and right sides of that center pillar, so we went to the left one, which was less busy. You could pay with col here, rather than chips, so Argo and I ordered ale, while Asuna and Liten ordered the sangria—which was red wine steeped with fruits and spices, apparently.

Our drinks came out in three seconds, so we shared a quick toast. It was nice and cool inside the casino, but even still, the ale had a pleasant chilling effect that refreshed my entire body. I would have preferred it to be nearly freezing, but ice was a luxury in Aincrad. I almost asked Argo about having another Snow Tree Bud, but it had a bit of a minty taste, which would clash with the ale.

I downed half the mug at once and exhaled with delight, as did Argo. Back on the first floor, I thought this stuff was just bitterly sour liquid, but at some point, I'd lost my resistance to the flavor and usually ordered it whenever it was available. I was going to have beer cravings if I ever got back to the real world.

Asuna and Liten downed their sangria, gulping noisily. The red wine with chopped fruit floating in it would normally have at least 10 percent alcohol content, but in this virtual world, you could drink an entire barrel of the stuff without suffering any kind of alcohol poisoning.

It was 10:20, ten minutes before the fifth and final match began. Hopefully we could learn what we wanted to hear by then.

I figured the best way to start would be to ask Liten, who was sitting across from Asuna on my right, what she thought of Volupta so far. But Argo, who was on Asuna's right, spoke up first.

"Hey, Li-chan, what's up with Kibaou and Lind getting so hooked on the monster battles? Neither of them's the type to put all their cash into gambling."

Why are you asking her right off the bat?! I thought in a panic, but Liten was not suspicious of the question in the slightest.

"That's right; I agree. But they're not just gambling recklessly without any kind of plan."

"Meaning?"

"The DKB came to the main town yesterday, as did we. Er, today? At one in the morning. We took inn rooms and met up at seven, ate breakfast, and went to the square, where there are two gates out of town. That's when an NPC came to talk to us."

"An NPC…? Was there supposed to be an event…?" wondered Argo. Asuna and I were confused as well. Presumably Liten was talking about where the statues of the man with the staff and the man with the goblet stood, but no NPCs came to speak with us there.

"Maybe that was a first-come, first-served event, then. It was a rather plain-looking man who asked us if we wanted to buy a cheat sheet for the Volupta monster coliseum."

"Cheat sheet?!" I blurted out, unable to believe what I was hearing. "He was totally ripping you off..."

"I thought so, too, and so did everyone else, I bet," Liten said, grimacing. She turned to Argo and continued, "The cheat sheet only cost a hundred col. That was all it cost for a list of every monster appearing in today's daytime and nighttime events, including their names, features, and even chances of winning. Plus a map to Volupta, a primer on the monsters on the way, even a guide to the town..."

"That sounds like quite a welcoming guide. This guy's gonna put me outta business. I was assuming there was another player out there who knew all about the casino. Instead, it's an NPC!" Argo wailed.

"Some of us thought it was suspicious that it cost so little, but Kiba said it was *worth a shot fer a pricey meal's cost...* We bought the cheat sheet and headed down the Tailwind Road. The map was accurate and so was the information on the monsters; we were in Volupta in no time. So we decided to try out the monster battle. We converted a thousand col into ten chips and put them all on the monster that the cheat sheet gave two circles for best chances. And we won. So we turned ten thousand col into a hundred chips for the next one and won again..."

Liten paused there to drink more sangria. Argo was deep in thought and decided to sound out what was on her mind. "Meanin' Kibaou and his pals kept betting on the better odds from the cheat sheet and winning big. Very nice for them."

"I suppose that NPC knows not to sell his cheat sheet to especially greedy players," needled Asuna.

I smiled at her and shot back, "That would mean you were included in that assessment."

"……"

I figured she was going to give me one of her usual rib jabs, but instead, she just beamed at me. "As evidence of my generosity, I'll give you this."

Then she picked up a big piece of citrus fruit from her glass of sangria and dropped it into my mug of ale.

"Hey, what was that for?!"

"Maybe it will make your drink taste better."

"No way…"

I lifted the mug to my lips, imagining spraying a poison mist attack in Asuna's face if it turned out to taste nasty—something that would mean my instant death. Instead, I swished it around for flavor.

"…Huh. It's not bad."

"See? I'm pretty sure there's a cocktail called a Bitter Orange, which is beer with orange juice added."

"You just thought of that off the top of your head," I accused.

On the other side of the table, Liten laughed. "Ah-ha-ha-ha. You really do make a good team."

"Oh, I w-wouldn't say that," Asuna claimed, clearing her throat and changing the subject. "Anyway…I'm guessing both the ALS and DKB were contacted by this man with the cheat sheet."

"Ah yes. When I saw him earlier tonight, Shiba said so," she mentioned, casually dropping the nickname for her boyfriend. Asuna was momentarily taken aback, losing the thread of the conversation, but she recovered quickly.

"Um…how many chips did you win through the previous match?"

"I think it was just over fifty thousand?"

That was a bit less than I expected, but it was probably because the cheat sheet didn't always recommend the monster with the higher odds.

"Meaning, if they bet on a monster with a double payout in the final match, they'll reach a hundred thousand chips," said Asuna.

Liten nodded. "That's right…but the group is arguing over

which one to bet on. In the fifth match, the sheet placed a circle on the monster with the better chance and a triangle on the one that's less likely. But the odds are about double for the triangle, and only one and a half for the circle..."

"And you've always been betting on the one with the better symbol?"

"Yes, yes. Some of the members lobbied for the less likely symbol up until about the third match during the day, but since all the results turned out like the cheat sheet said, they've been going strictly by the text tonight."

"Doesn't this seem...a bit too convenient?" I interjected. The gambler in me might have been annoyed, but my gamer senses were telling me something was suspicious about this. "Is it possible that a cheat sheet that costs a hundred col could be a hundred percent accurate about its picks...? Knowing how game events usually work, it could easily turn out that the very last match is the one where the other monster wins, and you lose everything you built up."

"Oh, Schinken said the same thing," Liten noted. I had to think for a moment before I realized she was talking about Schinkenspeck. According to Asuna, that was a type of ham made in Austria—not that it explained why he would have chosen that for a character name.

"Schinken said the last match might be a trap...and if we bet on the triangle mark that's worth twice as much, we'd have over a hundred thousand chips and be able to buy that sword with the incredible qualities. Ikura and Wälder agreed with Schinken... and that's when I left, so I don't know who they put our money on..."

"Um, who is Wälder?" I asked. I remembered Hokkai Ikura, but the other name was a new one, so I was curious.

Liten exhaled and took a deep breath. "Schwarzwälder Kirschtorte, officially. Another tank in our guild—and a long-standing member, too. It's only recently that Wälder really got the hang of the role and made it up to the first team."

"I see..."

Numerical aspects of the game like HP and skill proficiency would always rise if you kept working on them, but innate player skill was a different thing. And in a full-dive game, that kind of skill was even more important than in classic RPGs. The amount of time and effort one put into a single sword skill varied by the individual. Knowing what to do in a group fight required even more expertise—and being able to deal with a monster in your face—while tracking the state of your party members, guild members, and the battle as a whole was something that required knowledge, experience, and natural talent.

I'd always been a solo attacker focused on damage, so my player skill wasn't so great that I could speak as an authority on group battles. I was grateful to players like Wälder, who did their best to become first-rate warriors who could stand among the best. It was a very difficult name to remember, but that was a minor problem in the grand scheme of things.

I glanced down and to the right. The clock said 10:25, just five minutes until the fifth match. The ALS and DKB would have finished buying their ticket by now. In just moments, they would either seize glory or plunge into despair.

To be perfectly honest, I wanted to see that in real time, but it was a bit ghoulish of me. There was something else important we needed to ask Liten about.

"Thank you, Liten. That catches us up on the big competition between Lind and Kibaou. Hoping for the best for both of them. But I do have another question," I said.

Liten's face tightened up, and she nodded. "You must be referring to Buxum."

The three of us bobbed our heads. Buxum was a member of the PK gang and had been infiltrating the DKB. As an ALS member, Liten might not have ever met him, but in the meeting between the two guilds last night, Lind would surely have explained whatever he knew.

She drained the last of her sangria, took a deep breath, and said, "The DKB has more of a quality-over-quantity philosophy than us, but they're still openly recruiting new members. They're not scouting out anyone who will join like us, but they *are* handing out papers in the big towns on lower floors, and now and then they hold a membership assessment drive in the Town of Beginnings."

"Uh...huh..."

I'd never heard someone refer to the handouts as papers, rather than leaflets or flyers, but that wasn't important now.

"Assessment drive? What are they assessing?"

"That's what I asked Shiba. He said level, stats, and skill makeup on the first test, a demonstration of sword skills on the second test, and a duel with a guild member on the third test."

"*Third* test..." I muttered, the corner of my mouth twitching tensely.

"Are they even going to get anyone to apply?" asked Asuna, the skepticism wafting from her tone.

But Liten actually nodded. "There are more and more midrank players lately, and they want to break into the frontline group. They get twenty or thirty applicants each time, he said. A big part of that is that the DKB is the guild carrying on Diavel's dream. I haven't had the chance to talk to them myself, but apparently he's like a legendary hero to the players in the middle floors. Though Kibaou is a good leader, too."

The mention of his name caused me to remember Diavel the knight as I knew him. He perished in the battle against the first-floor boss on December 4, and today was January 5. It was impossible to believe it'd only been a month, but that was certainly enough time for him to become a legend among the midlevel players, I supposed.

Liten's voice broke the brief silence. "Buxum took part in an assessment drive at the end of December and fought Hafner to a duel in the third round of the test. That's when they decided to let him join the guild."

"End of December..." I repeated, constructing a mental timetable of our progress through Aincrad. The impromptu raid party of Asuna, Argo, Liten, and me beat the fifth-floor boss on the night of December 31. At the end of the year, nobody had any information about the quest series on the sixth floor. Beta testers were another story, but even in the test, the golden cube in the "Curse of Stachion" quest didn't have paralyzing powers.

So if Buxum was joining the DKB with the intent of stealing the golden cube from the start, the PK gang led by the man in the black poncho had to have gained information from some route other than a beta tester's knowledge.

"...Buxum, Morte, the dagger user in the black mask, and the man in the black poncho," Asuna said, counting them off on her fingers, which she clenched into a fist. "I wonder how many people are in that PK gang, total."

"I'm tryin' to get to the bottom of that myself, but I can't even find out where they gather..." Argo noted with frustration.

"Don't do anything too risky, Argo," Asuna told her. "They're dangerous and crafty. You have no idea where they could be lurking in wait."

She was right. We suspected that the PKer Asuna called the dagger user in the black mask might actually have been a senior member of the ALS named Joe, but we unfortunately had no hard evidence yet. I wanted to ask Liten about Joe, but if she realized we suspected him of foul play and confronted him directly, there was a possibility she could be singled out next.

"...What's wrong with them?" Liten grumbled, holding her empty glass with both hands. "PKing in the situation we're in. Interfering with our ability to beat the game is only prolonging our release from *SAO*..."

I couldn't answer that for her. Asuna and I had been tormented by the same question ever since we learned of their existence.

There just wasn't any *logic* behind the actions of the black poncho and his friends. But in a sense, that was one of their greatest advantages. The sheer irrationality of intentionally ruining a deadly game made it much harder to anticipate their actions.

I had to take a swig of orange-flavored ale to wash the bitterness from my mouth. From the right end of the table, I heard Argo say, "Do you know what the Bartle Test is?"

The other three of us shook our heads. The term was unfamiliar.

"It's something a game researcher created a long time ago. Basically, the idea is that you can classify all gamers into one of four types."

"Four types?" Liten repeated.

Argo held up a finger. "The first is Achievers. That's the type of player who tries to reach a goal set up within the game. Maxing out your level, getting all the best gear, finishing every quest, getting all the trophies."

I was never much for getting all the trophies, I thought, but I couldn't say it out loud before she held up a second finger.

"The second is Explorers, the folks who get excited fer exploring the unknown and finding out things on their own. Walking across every part of the world map, charging into dungeons and bosses you've never seen before, stubbornly trying to jump or climb up every wall and slope."

Ohhh, that might be me, I thought, but again I did not have time to say it out loud.

"The third is Socializers. These are the people who play games to socialize with others. They love playing cooperatively, running guilds, and just standing around on the map and chatting for hours."

This time, Asuna spoke up before I could even think of a comment. "That's the exact opposite of whatever Kirito is."

Liten made a bizarre *ffmrff* sound. Her head was pointed at the ground, so I could only assume she was holding back laughter. Argo briefly paused to smirk, then continued her lecture.

"And the fourth group is Killers. Those who derive enjoyment from killing other players."

The smiles vanished from Asuna's and Liten's faces. They froze, so I asked Argo, "Meaning...the PK gang is made of these Killers?"

"Well, I don't think it's meant to be that simple. I don't take the Bartle Test all that seriously, myself...but I think that out of all the players trapped in *SAO*, some of 'em are gonna have a real high resistance to PKing, and some are gonna have a lower resistance. The kind of folks who might just hop over that hurdle if the right thing gets whispered into their ear..."

Her voice was soft enough that I could just barely hear it at the other end of the table. Argo drained the rest of her mug, which was still half full.

Like Asuna and Liten, I was having trouble knowing what to say. If you needed to hear the right whispers in your ear, like Argo said...then how did the whisperer get over that hurdle in the first place? Unless it was the kind of person who had no resistance to killing someone else from the start.

It's showtiiiime.

The words replayed in my mind without my say-so, and my body tensed. Asuna must have sensed my chills, because she said very calmly, "This has been very useful information, Argo." Then she shrugged and smirked mischievously. "But I don't think I fit into any of the types."

I agreed with that. I mean, could you even define Asuna as a gamer?

But Argo just smiled and hissed through her teeth with laughter. "In that case, I propose a fifth category for you, A-chan. How about Progressors?"

""""Progressors?"""" the three of us said in unison.

"So...I'm making progress? Where am I going?"

"Wherever you should be progressing," said Argo, an evasive nonanswer to the question. From somewhere below, there was the distant sound of cheering. It seemed the fifth match had just begun.

"Are you heading back, Liten?" asked Asuna.

Liten considered this, then replied, "No...If they win, they'll come up here to exchange the chips for their prize, so I'll wait for them."

"Okay. Well, I think we'll move on, then."

"Don't you want to know the results?"

"If Kirito has to watch them claim that hundred-thousand-chip sword, he's going to weep with jealousy," Asuna said smugly, eliciting giggles and grins from Liten and Argo.

"I—I wouldn't weep!" I protested. "If anything, I'd just throw a little fit."

"That's plenty pathetic," Asuna said, rolling her eyes. I got to my feet along with her, but Argo stayed seated with Liten.

"I'll wait ta see the results. You two go back to the suite first."

"Okay, see you later, then. Thanks for talking with us, Liten."

"My pleasure. It was fun."

Asuna beamed and waved at them, and I held up my hand and closed it once as I left the counter. The cheers from the floor below rolled up like a wave at the shore. It seemed that the final bout was quite a showstopper.

"...If you *really* want to watch, I'll join you," Asuna said, walking toward the door. I grimaced.

"No, I'm fine. After what Nirrnir told us, I don't think I could enjoy watching the competition."

"That's true. By the way, Kirito, do you think she's...?"

She trailed off. I looked over, but Asuna just shook her head and said, "No, never mind."

Forty minutes later, when Argo returned to the Ambermoon Inn, we heard from her that both the ALS and DKB had lost their bets on the last match, and along with it, all of the fifty-thousand-plus chips they had won prior to it.

8

MY EYES DRIFTED OPEN, LIKE A DANDELION PUFF picked up on the breeze and falling back to earth.

The heavy lids opened just enough for me to glance at the time. It was two in the morning—only two hours since I'd gone to bed.

I wasn't the deepest sleeper in the real world, but strangely enough, I could completely knock out in Aincrad. Even I didn't know why I was able to sleep so soundly while trapped in a game that could kill me. Either the focus I needed to survive the day left me wiped out, or the device was shutting out all the extra sensations that would normally keep me from sleeping, or—as much as I didn't want to admit it—it was possible that I actually felt *comfortable* in this place.

So it was strange that I popped awake without a reason like this. I'd set my alarm for six o'clock, so I needed to sleep that extra four hours in preparation for the day ahead. I closed my eyes to go back to sleep—but then I felt a gentle shaking and frowned.

It was the vibration that had awakened me. Was it wind? An earthquake? A big wave? Or was Aincrad itself falling?

"Kirito, wake up," said a soft voice in my ear. I yelped and bolted upright. Or I would have, if I hadn't collided with something close to the bed. Purple light flashed in my eyes.

""Aurrg!"" said two voices together.

My head fell back to the pillow, where I blinked rapidly, trying to focus my eyes.

To the right of the bed, holding her hands to her temples, was my temporary partner. There was no real pain in this world, but when encountering phenomena that typically caused pain, your brain tried to create a kind of phantom sensation. The NerveGear was supposed to diminish even that phantom pain, but it couldn't stop you from imagining the pain from a sudden reaction like this.

So for the moment, Asuna and I groaned at the lingering effect of bonking our heads. Once we could look at each other again, I realized that the source of the shaking was not an earthquake or a gust of wind, but it had been her.

"...Um, what in the world...?" I asked.

The fencer grimaced and explained, "I kept calling your name, but you wouldn't wake up. So I had to shake you, and then you just jumped up out of bed."

"W-well, sorry about that...But why were you waking me up?"

"I was just thinking I'd like to leave a little bit early."

"Huh...?"

I had to check the clock again, thinking I'd read it wrong. But it was still two o'clock in the morning. The pale light coming through the crack in the window blinds belonged to the moon, not the morning sun.

"...More than a *little bit* early, don't you think?"

"I know...but I started thinking about things, and then I couldn't sleep," she murmured, sitting down on the edge of the bed. Her pale-blue nightclothes shone in the moonlight as though they were wet.

"...The 'Sacred Key' questline won't continue until we get to the dark elf base. I understand that. But Kizmel isn't just some program we can pause with the press of a button. She's got to sit around all alone at the base, waiting for us to arrive so the story can move forward again..."

"...That's true," I admitted, sitting upright.

Most likely, Asuna had arrived at this train of thought because we'd come in contact with NPCs on the sixth and seventh floors who were so expressive and reactive that they seemed to be real people. Myia, Theano, Bouhroum, and now Kio and Nirrnir. They were doing their best to live in this artificial world. And so was Kizmel, of course.

I didn't think Kizmel would be imprisoned for losing the four sacred keys to the Fallen Elves, but she wasn't going to be pampered for that failure. If she was in a painful situation, we needed to resume the quest for the six keys as soon as possible, to free her from that predicament.

However...

"You haven't slept a wink, have you, Asuna? I'm not thrilled about the idea of moving around an unfamiliar environment in the middle of the night, when you're short on sleep...Can't we at least get another hour of sleep?" I suggested.

But Asuna just waved her head from side to side. "No. This is one of those sleepless nights."

"Sleepless nights, huh...?"

I could understand that. I'd experienced wanting to go to sleep so badly (that the focus just kept you awake) many times before being trapped in *SAO*—and a few times since, too. *Oh well, as long as I'm watching out for her, I guess we'll be all right*, I thought, and was about to suggest that we get up and leave.

But then Asuna said, "Though I might be able to catch a *bit* of sleep." My mouth clamped shut, then opened again.

"Then in one hour, let's say, we should meet up in the living r—"

Before I had even finished my sentence, Asuna toppled to her right. She turned on her side, lifted her feet up onto the bed, grabbed a pillow and rested her head on it, then went still.

"......"

I stifled the inclination to ask her to go back to her own bedroom. If she was having trouble sleeping but feeling drowsy now, it would be cruel to interrupt her.

Plus, this wasn't the first time I'd slept very close to Asuna. If you played together as partners, there would be time when you needed to camp out and share a bedroll in the wilderness. You had to be used to this scenario.

I scooched over a tiny bit from the softly breathing girl, set my internal alarm to three o'clock, then stretched out on the bed.

Ten seconds later, I murmured silently, "This is one of those sleepless nights."

9

JANUARY 6, 3:10 AM.

My partner and I, back in our usual battle gear, walked side by side up the central stairs of Volupta.

The stores on either side of the street were shuttered tight, and not a single person could be seen walking along nearby. Things were probably still bustling on the western staircase, with all the shady bars, and there might have even been some late-night quest prompts there, but this was not the time for detours.

Despite leaving nearly three hours ahead of time, we were still pushing our luck with the schedule we'd set up for ourselves. First, we'd go to Looserock Forest in the center of the floor, meet up with Kizmel at the dark elf base, then collect twenty narsos fruits while advancing the "Sacred Key" questline. We'd have to return to Volupta by noon. Either we'd have to pause the key quest at that point and ask Kizmel to wait at her base, or else she'd be coming into Volupta with us.

Even with Argo handling the wurtz stone collection, it was a lot to do. Just thinking about it brought the last vestiges of sleepiness forward, and I let out a huge yawn. Asuna, who was walking briskly along, leaned forward so she could look up at me from below.

"You slept three times as much as I did, and you're still sleepy?"

"It wasn't three times as much. Maybe two and a half," I said, because I couldn't very well say, *I couldn't sleep at all because you fell asleep in my bed.* "And how are you so wide awake if you only slept for an hour?"

"Hmm, I dunno. That one hour has me feeling pretty good."

"…Well, good for you, milady," I said. Asuna shot back with, "Thank you, manservant." She was probably feeling hyped up not because of the lack of sleep but from the anticipation of meeting Kizmel very soon.

I was looking forward to that, too, of course. But we were already on the seventh floor of Aincrad. The "Elf War" campaign quest started on the third floor, and it would end on the ninth. We had maybe two or three weeks, at the most, left to go on adventures with her.

But even after the questline, we should be able to see Kizmel anytime, as long as we descended to the ninth floor. So I didn't need to mention any depressing facts to bring down Asuna. It was hard enough to find things to look forward to in this deadly game; might as well appreciate them while we had them.

For some reason, I heard a phantom version of Argo's mischievous "nee-hee-hee" laugh, and I shivered. She was still fast asleep in her bedroom, so we left her a note, but I was certain she'd have some teasing to do when we met around midday. I needed to prepare for that and have some witty comebacks ready.

I was simulating that conversation in my immature, eighth-grade mind when Asuna said, "I wonder what Lind and Kibaou are going to do."

"Do?"

"They didn't win their bet on the final match and lost everything they had, right?"

"It's not *everything* they had," I said with a chuckle. "According to Liten, the first ALS bet was eleven thousand col. That's a lot of money, but when the DKB members were trying to buy the guild flag from us, they offered three hundred thousand. The ALS probably has about as much, so if they came out of that losing eleven thousand, well, that's just the price of a valuable lesson, don't you think?"

"The price of a lesson…" Asuna repeated, frowning. "So does this mean the NPC man who sold Lind and Kibaou the cheat sheet was actually a scammer?"

"I don't think I'd call him that…The cheat sheet was only a hundred col, and its suggestions were correct on nine out of the ten matches yesterday. So it was probably intended to build up trust through the first nine matches, then get them to bet as big as possible in the tenth and lose. That wouldn't make him a scammer—but a plant from the casino, perhaps."

"Hmmm…" Asuna didn't seem entirely convinced by my interpretation. She turned her head the other way. "But the monster arena isn't like the roulette or card tables. The bettors are wagering their money against one another, right? Lady Nirrnir said the only money the casino makes on those is from the ten percent fee on each ticket purchase. So if Kibaou's group lost tens of thousands of col, it would be the other visitors to the casino who made that money. The casino only gets a small bit of that."

"That's exactly correct," I said, impressed by how quickly she grasped the concept. "So if my imagination is accurate, one or more of those bettors are actually with the casino. They bet on the opposite of Kibaou's pick, so that if they win, they win big."

"That's so dirty!" Asuna blurted out, pulling no punches. "But…that means they can manipulate the outcome of the matches, right? So wouldn't it be impossible unless the trainers of both monsters…meaning Bardun Korloy and Nirrnir, work together, right…?"

"Not necessarily," I said, having considered this just seconds earlier. I did my best to explain. "If only one of the two is acting improperly, it might be tricky to guarantee a win, but you can certainly guarantee a loss. You could choose the weakest monster in the specified rank and weaken it further with poison before the fight. Then you write in the cheat sheet that you expect your monster to win—and trick Kibaou into betting big on you."

"Even still, that doesn't add up. The cheat sheet had a favorite for each of the nine matches before that, and they were all correct. I assume not all the losers were the Korloys' monsters. They'd need to win a few......Ah!"

When she gasped, I nodded slowly. "Yes, they probably engaged in some cheating in order to win, too. One of those attempts was the dye trick with the Rusty Lykaon. I bet the other matches that the Korloy family's monsters won had some kind of cheating in effect—we just didn't notice it. That way, they not only get the cut from the matches they win, but they also get money when they lose."

"......So in every one of the matches, it's uh, what do you call it...? When only one side is cheating..."

"When one side is losing on purpose, that's called throwing the match. But the Korloys are also cheating in order to win."

"I see...Well anyway, it's dirty. Nirrnir's trying her best to fulfill her role, but the Korloys are cheating for no reason other than increasing their profit," my partner said, fuming.

I was going to tell her that was just part of the quest background, but I swallowed my words. A month ago, I would have considered this Bardun Korloy to be nothing but a cog in a story written by a game writer in the real world. But Kizmel, Myia, Theano, and even Kysarah, the Fallen Elf adjutant who stole the sacred keys, seemed to be acting of their own free will. It was possible that Bardun was merely placed in a situation and had made all subsequent choices on his own.

Nirrnir said Bardun was gathering as much money as he could to buy a small amount of life, with no other concerns. If that wasn't just a simple bit of characterization, then what was it that made him fear death so much? And what exactly did she mean by "buying life" with money...?

"Kirito, there's the exit."

I looked up and saw a smaller gate ahead of us. At some point, we'd finished climbing the central stairs and reached the square on the northern end of Volupta.

The gate was wide open, despite the hour, and while there were guards on either side, their heads were lolling sleepily. I couldn't blame them for being bored; whether they took their job seriously or not, the monsters outside the town were physically prevented from getting inside by the game system. In a sense, this had to be the emptiest job imaginable.

Out of an abundance of sympathy, I actually said "Good evening" as we passed them. One of the guards seemed to be sleeping on his feet, but the other one lifted his head and said, "It's dangerous at night. Be careful." Asuna smiled and thanked him.

We passed through the elegant but sturdy gate and headed out into the wilderness. The words LEAVING TOWN appeared, then vanished.

I sucked in a deep breath of night air blowing across the plains ahead and stretched as far as I could.

Asuna gave me a funny look and asked, "Did you always used to greet the town guards?"

"No, just…every now and then…"

"Mm-hmm. He totally jumped; did you see that? I bet he thought he was going to get yelled at by his boss for sleeping on the job," she said with a giggle.

It occurred to me that I should probably greet the guards more often in the future. We set off down the road out of town by moonlight.

Aincrad's seventh floor was split into flatlands on the southern side and mountains on the north. The roads from the main town to the labyrinth tower both curved their way around through those environs, so hardly any players—or NPCs—bothered to set foot in the center.

Because of that, the road heading directly north from Volupta quickly showed cracks in the paving stones and turned into simple exposed dirt shortly thereafter. When it rained on this surface, the mud could make it easier to tumble, but we didn't need to worry about that for a while.

We made our way forward carefully, dispatching the moths and stag beetle monsters that replaced the bees and lancer beetles from the day. I was pretty sure that all kinds of rhinoceros beetles were nocturnal in the real world, but these insects were nearly half a meter long, so expecting perfect realism was perhaps beside the point.

After thirty minutes of walking, the environment began to change. The short grass that covered the gentle slopes began to get thicker, and there were more trees about. Eventually, we saw especially large broadleaf trees framing the path ahead.

A clammy headwind blew past us, and the trees rustled loudly. It was practically warning us, *"Danger ahead!"* You didn't need to be in a game of death to recognize that this area called for caution.

I opened my mouth to warn Asuna, but she beat me to the punch.

"Aspens."

"…Wh-what?"

I started looking around, wondering, *Was that a monster on the seventh floor? Where are they?* But there was no hint of a monster's presence and no red cursors. I kept looking, until Asuna snapped, "It's not a monster. It's the name of those trees."

"Huh…?" I looked up at the pair of trees that stood watch over the path. "They're called aspens? Are they real trees?"

"Real trees. Their leaf-cluster density is high, so they make a lot of noise when the wind blows. That's why they're also called quaking aspens. And the traditional Japanese name is mountain sounders."

"Hmm, I may have heard of that before. That reminds me, you guessed the name of the trees at Yofel Castle on the fourth floor, too."

"That was because Kizmel mentioned they were junipers first. I only knew the Japanese name," Asuna remarked, smiling very slightly. It disappeared, probably because the thought made her worry for Kizmel again. I wanted to hurry onward, but there was other danger ahead aside from monsters.

"Well, we're about to enter Looserock Forest, but I need to warn you…"

"About the loose rocks?" she asked. I could only nod.

"Yeah, them."

"Sorry, sorry!" Asuna chuckled and patted my arm. "What exactly does it mean that the rocks are loose?"

"Well…"

I formed a sphere in the air with my hands, trying to explain with my limited vocabulary.

"The floor of Looserock Forest is wetland, so it's hard to walk, and here and there the water goes really deep. There's a path made of these huge boulders, but sometimes they just rock beneath your feet. It's about five to ten feet from the top of the rocks to the ground, and because the ground is covered in water, you barely take any damage, but it's really hard to get back up on the rock. Plus, when you walk in the swamp…Well, at any rate, you'll be able to recognize the loose rocks if you watch closely, so let's just pay attention, shall we?"

I started to walk again, finished with my explanation, when Asuna grabbed my arm and held me back this time.

"Stop right there."

"Wh-what?"

"You just skipped over something. *When you walk in the swamp…*what? What comes after that?"

"……Ummm," I muttered awkwardly, thinking fast. But I knew well enough by now that I couldn't pull the wool over my partner's eyes. "In the marsh water, there are some bottomless holes, like I mentioned, plus some translucent, slimy, frilly guys that look like *melibe viridis*…Do you know what *melibe viridis* is?"

"……I do not," said Asuna very carefully, her face a tapestry of rich emotion.

I rested my hand on her shoulder. "Then you can look it up when we get back to the real world. As long as you don't fall off the rocks, you won't have to worry about them."

"……I'll do that," she said. I gave her a quick smile and resumed traveling.

Past the two aspens was a small hill, followed by a dark line of trees. Within that forest was the dark elf fortress. The enemy forest elf base was near the outer perimeter on the northwest part of the floor, beyond some treacherous mountains. It was quite a trek, but of course, we had no reason to visit.

The hour was four o'clock. Lots of time until sunrise.

Following my line of thought, Asuna said, "It's dark in the forest. Should we get out a torch?"

"No, we won't need one…I think."

"Why not?"

"You'll see when we get inside the forest."

Asuna made a face at that unhelpful answer, but she changed her expression once we reached the trees.

The boundary line between the Verdian Plains we'd just crossed and Looserock Forest was so sharp and stark that it could never happen in real life. At the other end of the hill, there was a wall of trees nearly seventy feet tall, with a darkened entrance between them so obvious it looked like the mouth of a dungeon. The path wound its way through that gap, and there was no visible light beyond it whatsoever.

"…Are you *sure* we won't need light?"

"Just wait," I reassured her, taking us down the slope and through the gap in the trees. The moonlight behind us got dimmer, and we were soon surrounded by darkness so thick that you couldn't see more than six feet in front of you. The temperature was dropping significantly, until the summer night humidity completely vanished.

At this point, almost any player would light a torch or lantern. I did that during the beta. But this time, I continued walking through the thick line of trees, grappling with the primordial fear of darkness.

Eventually, our footsteps turned from the dry scraping of earth into the sharper impact of something harder. The ground under

our feet turned from dirt to rock. Along with the two sets of footsteps came the sound of running water.

"......Ah," Asuna gasped. There was a faint green light up
ahead. As we got closer, it became clear that the illumination was
coming from some mushrooms growing on the trunks of the
trees. There were bioluminescent mushrooms in the real world,
but these were larger and brighter.

Asuna came to a stop before a glowing fungus, a round cap that
looked like a light bulb, and tapped it. The window that appeared
displayed the name BONFIRE SHROOM.

"Bonfire shroom...That's not a real mushroom, right?" Asuna
asked, turning to me.

"Not as far as I know."

"When it says bonfire, is it referring to the big bonfires they
light for Obon, to send the spirits of the dead on their way? Like
the one in Kyoto."

"I'm assuming so..."

In other words, this mushroom was glowing to help guide the
spirits who'd briefly returned to the living world back to the land
of the dead. Not the most auspicious name, but if they weren't
here, it would be instantly three times as hard to get through
Looserock Forest.

Asuna straightened up and exclaimed again, softly and word-
lessly. Ahead, there were two more green glowing lights that
hadn't been there before.

As she reached them, more lights appeared, as though guiding
us along. If you didn't know what these were, you might think it
was a trap, but the mushrooms were not doing anything of their
own will or according to any great plan. They simply reacted by
glowing whenever a player or NPC approached—and when any
other nearby specimens glowed.

For several minutes, we walked alongside the soft green light,
until suddenly, the trees gave way on either side. The bonfire
shrooms' guidance ended, too, leaving nothing but utter darkness ahead.

"...Huh? Are we already through the forest? We've only been walking a few minutes," said Asuna with consternation.

I held up my right hand to stop her. "Hang on a moment."

"Okay..."

We stood still, waiting.

Then, on our right up ahead, a bonfire shroom lit up.

In reaction, a cluster of them shone farther away. Then another group. The chain reaction of luminescence continued without end, until the lights were nearly as numerous as the sky at night. A vast space was lit by a pale green glow.

"Wowww!" Asuna exclaimed, stepping forward. I had to quickly grab the sleeve of her tunic.

Before us was a natural corridor, built of massive trees and their thick foliage. The corridor was roughly a hundred feet tall and across, and it was impossible to tell how far it went. We were standing atop pillars of rock with flat tops, and the ground ten feet below was covered with clear water and aquatic plants. The canopy of so many thick branches overhead dangled a plethora of vines, through which large butterflies flapped lazily.

The rock pillars ran in a line through the center of the passageway of trees and water, twisting and turning as it went. The sight of all this, lit by the unearthly green color of the bonfire shrooms, was nothing short of ethereal.

Once I was sure my partner was standing still with wonder, I let go of her tunic and removed a torch from my inventory. When Asuna noticed that, she seemed almost affronted.

"Wait...It's so bright now. Do we really need that?"

"Just watch."

I tapped the torch with my free hand to activate it. The moment the orange flames arose, the light of the nearest group of bonfire shrooms went out. That phenomenon rapidly spread, until the entire tunnel of green was completely dark in the span of under ten seconds. Only deep darkness surrounded us, with nothing but a few meters of light against the rock pillars to guide us.

"I see…So the shrooms don't activate if there's other light nearby," Asuna murmured.

I tapped the burning torch and said, "Exactly. So if you light your torch right at the entrance to the forest, you'll never find out the mushrooms glow, and you'll have to work your way through the forest in this darkness. Not that it would be impossible…"

I hit the EXTINGUISH button on the window, and the torch's flames quickly dwindled, then went out.

Within a few seconds, the nearest batch of bonfire shrooms glowed again. The luminescence spread quickly and quietly, until the entire corridor was again lit a ghostly green.

My demonstration finished, I stashed the torch away and pointed to the string of rock pillars we were standing on.

"These are the loose rocks the dungeon is named after. And you'll find the loose ones, oh…every seventh rock or so."

"How loose are we talking here?" Asuna asked, prodding at the rock under her feet with the toe of her boot.

I recalled the general experience from the beta. "Uhhh…it's not a *hurp*! More like, somewhere between a *wubble* and a *rumba*."

"……Without using sound effects."

"Uhhhh…Once you know it's loose, you can plant your feet and still maintain your balance."

"How can you tell if it'll be a loose one?"

"It's hard to explain with words, so I'll just point it out to you," I said, moving to the next rock. Asuna followed, rather timidly.

The circular pillars were all an even ten feet above the water, but there was significant variety in their size. The smallest ones were less than two feet across, while the biggest ones were over four feet. The problem was that the size didn't necessarily correspond to stability.

"This one's fine…This one's fine, too…" I said out loud, crossing from pillar to pillar. Five, six—and I was just about to step on the seventh.

"Aha. Here's one."

I pulled back the leg I had extended forward, then crouched down.

"Here, look at this," I said, pointing out the seam between pillars. The other pillars were completely seamless where they met, but the seventh was just a bit separate from the previous. It was only a few centimeters or so, which meant you might not notice it unless you were focusing on it right as you got there.

"The ones that are just a bit separated from the others are the loose rocks. There are other identifying features, but they're really subtle, so just looking for the gaps is the best way to go."

"...Got it."

"I'll step on it first. You watch how I keep balance."

"Y-you're going to be all right?"

"Totally fine."

I think, I added silently. I spread out my hands and stepped forward.

The diameter of the loose rock was a bit over two feet. I set my boot down right along the middle and carefully shifted my weight forward. When I was half resting on the rock, I could feel it begin to tilt to the right. It was like standing on a stake that was only lightly struck into soft earth. In fact, that might essentially describe what this rock was.

Carefully adjusting my center of balance, I went ahead and placed all my weight on my right foot. The rock continued to tremble, but it wasn't leaning far either way. I slowly brought my left foot forward, focusing on balancing with all my concentration, and placed it along the center line, too. Then I transferred my weight to the left foot, lifted the right, and set it down on the next rock.

"There..."

I pulled my left foot forward, then exhaled slowly. I was hopping all over these things in the beta, but four months later, I seemed to have lost the knack of it. There would be plenty of these to cross, so I resigned myself to relearning the basics.

"Ah, I see. Give me room," Asuna declared from two rocks

away, so I moved another rock forward, then turned back to watch.

"Think you can make it?"

"The trick is to keep your weight in the center of the rock, right?" Asuna said. She didn't sound particularly concerned.

She placed her left foot on the loose rock. That made me wonder if the right foot was my dominant foot, while Asuna's was the left. No sooner had the thought entered my mind than Asuna quickly alternated feet and crossed the rock without any perceptible wobbling. She stopped in the middle of my rock and grinned.

"What's my score?"

"I'll give you ninety-nine points."

"…Why did I lose one?"

"You showed up the teacher," I said.

She snorted and looked at the next pillar. "Oh…The next one's loose, too?"

"Hmm…? Oh, you're right."

Down at my feet, there was a very slight gap between our pillar and the next one in the line.

"What happened to the loose rocks being once every seven?"

"I—I was only talking averages. Sometimes you have little clusters of them, and sometimes you don't see any for a while."

"I knew that. Anyway, I'll go first."

"Be my guest," I said, taking two steps to the side. I looked at the ceiling of the corridor.

The monster-spawning rate in Looserock Forest was very low, but it wasn't zero. Every now and then, a giant dragonfly or giant stick bug or giant skyfish floated down from the canopy, and if it happened while you were trying to cross a loose rock, it could cause a brief panic.

But for now, there were only a few giant butterflies floating around, which were neutral mobs that didn't attack unless you did. I looked forward again and saw Asuna unsteadily crossing a loose rock.

She took four steps to cross a larger rock than the first one and was just hopping to the next one when I noticed something.

"…!"

I had to stop myself from shouting. If it startled her, that would only make things worse. I just had to pray she noticed it herself.

The next rock was *also* loose.

Asuna landed with a soft thump, then took a big step to the right, probably to make room for me to follow. The rock lurched to the side.

"Asuna!"

This time I shouted, right as she blurted out "Huh?!"

Asuna tried her best to balance, but the rock tilted at least twenty degrees, hurtling her into empty air.

My heart seized up, and my limbs went cold. But she would still be fine—the ground below was merely swamp with a water cover of a foot and a half, so it would absorb the fall damage, and she couldn't drown in it. As long as she didn't happen to land on one of the bottomless holes.

Despite the shock of the experience, Asuna did not scream. She maintained bodily control in the air and stretched out her limbs as she landed. There was a deep but quiet splash when she hit the water, knees bent to absorb the impact. The display of her HP bar did not lose a single pixel.

"Whew……"

Relieved, I called out to my partner.

"Asuna, you okay?!"

The fencer was still, not moving from her landing position. Slowly, she straightened up and looked at me. "I'm fine…but my butt got wet."

"Ah. Well, it'll dry off once you're out of the water. Don't move; I'll lower a rope."

"Got it," she said, scowling but giving me a thumbs-up. I flashed one back, then opened my player menu.

At least three times during the beta, I fell off these rocks. In order to get back up as a solo player, you had to return all the way to the entrance of the corridor and walk up a cramped staircase carved into the rock. But with a party, you could get your companions to lift you up.

I materialized my Nephila-string rope, which was strong enough to hold the weight of three players without breaking, then made a loop on the end so I could toss it down to Asuna.

But at that moment, she uttered a soft "Eek!" and pulled her arms up to her chest, standing stock-still.

"Wh-what's wrong?!"

"S…something touched my leg…"

I scrambled to the edge of the rock and leaned over to look down at her feet. The light of the bonfire shrooms was strong enough to guide you across the rock bridge, but it couldn't shine into the water below.

Still, I squinted hard, watching the shifting surface of the water, then saw a shape slip past Asuna's boot. A moment later, a color cursor appeared. It was a very light shade of pink, and the name was HEMATOMELIBE.

I let out a bit of the breath I was holding and shouted, "Don't move, Asuna! The monster is gross, but alone, it poses almost no danger!"

"*Almost*…? Ah, *yeep!*" she squawked, because the hematomelibe began slithering up her right leg.

It was a long, narrow invertebrate, about twenty inches long. The body was translucent, and you could see a black digestive tract down its center. A number of waving finlike protuberances lined its back, and many long feelers extended from its head.

"Wha…?! No, no, no, I can't do this!" she screamed, leaning backward for all she was worth—but she didn't try to peel it off. Or maybe she couldn't. In any case, she'd just have to bear it for the moment.

After the first time I encountered this monster in the beta, I searched the name *hematomelibe*. It didn't turn up any direct matches, but breaking it into separate words gave me the gist of it. *Melibe* was the name of a genus of sea slugs. *Hemato* was a prefix meaning *blood*. So combining the two formed the name blood slug.

Further searching taught me about the actual sea slug called *melibe viridis*, which I'd mentioned to Asuna earlier. The hemato-melibe in Aincrad was clearly named after *melibe viridis*, and the *hemato* prefix was very relevant, indeed.

"I can't! I can't! I can't do thiiis!" she screeched as the giant sea slug came to a stop about six inches above her knee. The multitude of feelers on its head writhed against her leg, searching the skin between her tall boots and skirt.

"Hya…!"

"Hang in there a bit longer! It's only going to suck a little blood!" I reassured her.

This had the opposite of its intended effect.

"M…mnyaaaaaaa!!"

Her scream reached every length of the forest corridor. Asuna grabbed the back of the hematomelibe with her bare hand, then ripped it off with all her strength and slammed it against the rock pillar next to her.

The translucent body burst with a disgusting *shplack!* The visible digestive tract ripped in two, oozing a reddish-black liquid into the swamp water. The ugly remnants of the creature stuck to the rock surface turned to blue particles and dispersed.

Of all the monsters on the seventh floor, the hematomelibe was by far the weakest. It had almost no defense and just a pittance of hit points. Its only attack method was very slow bloodsucking. If you ignored the fact that they were very gross, there was nothing to fear from them—when they were alone.

"Uh-oh…"

Without a moment's hesitation, I jumped off the pillar. I landed with a larger splash than Asuna made and called out, "Are you all right, Asuna?!"

"Y-yeah," she admitted, then blinked twice with surprise and suspicion. "Um…Why did you jump down here, too? Who's going to get us back up there?"

"Gotta start over from the beginning. Let's hurry!"

I grabbed her hand and turned, then clicked my tongue with irritation. Three more light-pink cursors were floating above the water, gliding toward us. They belonged to three more hemato-melibe, of course.

"Kirito, they're coming from the right, too...and behind us!" Asuna cried.

I let go of her hand. "They're drawn by the blood of the one that just died. Forget moving. We've got to fight!"

"But if we just beat the three ahead of us..."

"It's impossible to aim at them while they're in the water. Once you start struggling, dozens of them will swarm you, until you can't stay upright from the weight. At that point, you could easily drown, even in this shallow water," I explained as quickly as possible. Asuna didn't argue any further; she just said, "Got it."

We drew our swords and stood with our backs to the line of rock pillars. At least this way, we could limit the slugs' attack to three sides.

"They go into a frenzy over their own kind's blood, so they'll jump out of the water and try to attach to you. You've got to take them in order. Only use a sword skill if more than one is striking at the same time."

"Got it!" she repeated, right as the surface of the water burst on our right.

Two bloodsucking slugs, their back fins spread out like wings, leaped toward us. I hit one with a diagonal slash, while Asuna thrust directly into the other. The weak invertebrates split in two, just from the ordinary weapon attacks, and fell into the water before dispersing into particles.

Another two hematomelibe jumped at us. Again, we easily cut them down. Asuna murmured, "If they're drawn by the blood of their own kind, then won't they just keep coming, the more of them we kill?"

"Pretty much...Whoa!"

On my left, two cursors leaped in succession. I carefully

identified the locations of the two and lined up the single-slash Vertical skill to dispatch them. Another single slug jumped at Asuna, and she destroyed it with a blindingly fast thrust.

Normally, bludgeoning attacks were most effective against invertebrates like the hematomelibe, and the effect got steadily worse with slashing, thrusting, and puncturing damage, in that order. My Sword of Eventide was a slashing weapon, so it did decent damage, but Asuna's Chivalric Rapier was piercing, so its lethality with normal attacks was less certain.

But because it was originally a strong weapon and had been boosted to +7 by the dark elf blacksmith, her weapon from the third floor still boasted superlative power here on the seventh. As evidence of that, she turned the bloodsucking slug into a circle with a hole in the middle. And to think the rapier still had another eight upgrade attempts on it.

What would it be like if all eight were successful, and it became a +15 weapon? I wanted to see that, but the thought also made me nervous. Not because I was imagining ever crossing weapons with Asuna, of course. But a weapon with such potentially broken stats would be coveted by the front-runners...not to mention the PK gang...

"Aaahh...Here comes a bunch of them!" Asuna screeched, focusing my attention on the surface of the water again. Over twenty cursors were approaching from the distance.

"It's the same process! If one of them attaches itself to you, don't panic; just peel them off and smack them against the wall behind us. As long as we don't panic, we'll easily survive this!" I stated authoritatively.

That helped reassure Asuna. "Got it. I wanna talk to you about something after this."

I didn't even have time to wonder what it was. The water splashed up ahead, and more bloodsucking sea slugs came leaping toward us. We fought them off with slashes and thrusts.

The mirror-bright rapier left faint zigzag aftereffects in the darkness. Her thrusts were so fast that the reflective light ran together into a solid beam.

Asuna's strength as a player wasn't all due to the specs of the Chivalric Rapier. With each floor we traversed, Asuna's skill in combat evolved dramatically. I was more often in the teaching role simply because of the gap in our relative knowledge about the monsters of *SAO*—and how its game systems worked—but in a couple of floors, say, the tenth or so, she would have made up that ground.

With each flash of her rapier, another hematomelibe disintegrated in midair as a hollowed tube. There was no way you could cause that effect to a blobby invertebrate unless you pierced them exactly head-on down the middle. It took superb concentration, physical control, and affinity for the full-dive experience to achieve this kind of mastery.

Asuna wasn't meant to be the partner of an outcast like me. She was destined to shine on a much larger stage.

While that wasn't necessarily a new feeling, something else rose in me that was. It was a kind of hesitation, perhaps a fixation. I wanted to be able to watch her skill grow right beside me. I didn't want to let anyone else have her. In the real world, I kept my distance from everyone and even shunned my family to an extent. It was ironic that it took getting trapped in a virtual world for me to feel this for the first time.

A third of my brainpower was occupied by these thoughts, as I cut through hematomelibe up, down, left, right, and center. When I fell into this exact same situation in the beta, I felt my willpower getting ground down by waves of enemies with no sign of letting up, but having gone through the experience, I knew that if you withstood the rush, they *would* run out eventually. Plus, I had a very reliable partner to help me fight.

For the first few minutes, we called out locations to each other for assistance, but eventually we stopped needing to do that. Asuna and I caught little glimpses of each other's movements out of the corner of our eyes and listened for the soft sound of our breathing to anticipate the timing of the other's attack and offer backup, as we steadily fought off invaders on three sides.

Eventually, we grew numb to panic, fear, and even the passage of time. I was swinging my sword in a trance—and the next thing I knew, the color cursors that seemed to have buried the surface of the water were all gone, like a vanished mirage.

Still, I stood with my sword at the ready, allowing my mind to empty for several moments, and finally I relaxed. At my side, Asuna's eyes had a dazed, far-off look to them. She blinked a few times and focused on me.

"......It's over?"

"......I think."

I glanced around several times, just to be sure. The fencer examined the rapier in her hand, then said, "I'm glad they were soft monsters. I didn't lose much durability."

"Y-yeah...True. I wonder how many we beat..."

"I stopped counting at fifty."

There wasn't much to our conversation, but it was a decent way to let our nerves unwind. I shook my head to clear the trance state from my mind.

"Anyway, nice job. You did great," I said, holding up my fist. Asuna touched her knuckles to mine.

"Same to you, Kirito. Also...I'm sorry."

"For what?"

"For not following your instructions. If I'd stayed still like you said with the first one, it wouldn't have resulted in that huge swarm," she said, surprisingly deflated.

"N-no, that wasn't your fault," I quickly insisted. "If I'd warned you about what the hematomelibe looks like, and what it does..."

Then I remembered what Asuna had said just before the fight started.

"...Wait, is that what you wanted to talk to me about afterward?" I asked. Immediately, the fencer's regal and gracious attitude evaporated with a puff of steam.

"Oh…yes! That! I'm sure you didn't say anything because you thought I would find it gross— Well, stop doing that! I'll admit, I may have no natural resistance to gross-type monsters, but I'm not going to tell you we should turn back on account of it!"

"…Can I tell you about the ghost monsters, too?"

"*Nmlp…*"

She made a sound like something getting stuck in her throat, but eventually, she gave up and nodded awkwardly.

"Y-yes, you can. It's better than coming face-to-face without having any advance warning. By the way…do *they* show up here, too?"

"They…do………"

I held it there for three seconds, then made a giant X with my forearms.

"…not!"

Asuna punched my shoulder—with her left hand—just softly enough that it didn't cause damage.

With the sea slugs gone, we sloshed through the swamp back to the entrance of the forest corridor. Climbing the stairs carved into the wall, we started the balancing act again upon the rocks.

The number of loose rocks had increased since the beta test. Not only did they come two in a row, every now and then it was three in a row. But as long as we walked down the center of each rock, it wasn't too hard to maintain balance, thanks to our light weight. When the flying insect monsters came down to harass us, it was easy enough to stand on firm rocks and throw stones at them. After about twenty minutes, our destination was within view.

"Wowwww!!" Asuna exclaimed, even more enthusiastically than the first time she'd seen the corridor lit up.

I couldn't blame her. If you were making a list of the hundred greatest views in Aincrad, this would have to be one of them.

Our south corridor was converging with others from the north, east, and west, into a rounded dome. In the center of the dome was a proud, mammoth tree, at least a hundred and fifty feet across. The monster baobab trees from Zumfut on the third floor were about a hundred feet, so if you cut them down, the cross section would be nearly three times bigger for this one.

If you told me this tree was a thousand years old, I would believe it. A large knot in the tree yawned near the roots, with a wooden door set just behind it. There were also many, many open holes around the trunk, with greenish light spilling out of them. Like the baobabs in Zumfut, this tree was hollow, with living quarters inside it.

Asuna just stood and stared in wonder. I leaned over and murmured, "That's the dark elf base on the seventh floor, Harin Tree Palace."

We crossed the last hundred meters of the rock bridge and jumped to a large cluster of rock pillars clumped together in a honeycomb pattern. At last, we could relax.

On other sides of the platform were other rock bridges that led to the other forest corridors. Ahead of us was the knot hollow that was the main gate to Harin Tree Palace, standing nearly thirty feet high. The gate just behind the opening was made of different types of wood fit into a herringbone pattern like a gigantic work of art.

"And Kizmel's...in there..." Asuna murmured.

I pushed her lightly on the back. "C'mon, let's go. I'm sure she's waiting for us."

"...Yeah."

As she walked forward, I checked the time. It was 5:07 AM, nearly two hours after we'd left Volupta. If we turned back at the swamp entrance, then it would be a three-hour round trip, just like Nirrnir said.

Our quest objective, the narsos fruit, was growing somewhere in the wetland here. We had the option of continuing to search for the fruit after we got down and fought those hematomelibe, but Asuna didn't want any more detours, I figured, and I wanted to see Kizmel, too.

We quickly crossed the rocky platform and stopped at the roots of the tree palace. This close, all you could see when you looked up was a trunk so vast it was like a giant wall—and the branches far, far overhead.

"...I wonder what the widest tree is in the real world and how big it is..." I said absentmindedly.

I didn't expect an answer, but Asuna immediately said, "It's the Árbol del Tule in Mexico, if I recall correctly. I'm pretty sure the diameter is close to fifty feet at the base."

"I...I can't believe you know that. Fifty feet across is amazing, but I feel like this one is at least three times that size."

"I agree...If we ask Kizmel, she'll probably tell us the history, won't she?"

"Yeah, I bet."

We shared a brief look, then proceeded onward again.

The rock path led us between roots that were over twice our height, right up to the gate. Fire stands lined the path, but the light coming from the cages at the top was not the orange of flames but a pale green. They were cultivating the bonfire shrooms as a light source.

The trail led us through the hollow in the tree. The herringbone-pattern door was right before us. The two gates were shut perfectly tight, and I suspected they would not open even if we pushed them.

I didn't see any guards around, and unlike with Castle Galey on the sixth floor, nobody called out to us for identification while we waited outside.

"Hmm, that's weird...When I came here in the beta, I remember the gates opening just from walking up to them," I murmured, frowning. Asuna ran out of patience and stepped forward, raising her left hand high to show off the large Sigil of Lyusula ring on her pointer finger.

"We are human warriors assisting Kizmel of the Pagoda Knights Brigade of Lyusula! We have come to this land to see her! Please open the gates!"

This was a proper introduction for following the story of a quest. My partner was growing into quite the VRMMO player.

There was a deep rumble, and the huge gates slowly opened to the sides. We had avoided being shut out at the door, to my relief. As they opened, I watched the gates closely. It wasn't just the surface; the inner structure was wooden, too, and even the gears that helped them open and close. The elves couldn't cut down living trees, so they must have collected all this material from dead or fallen trunks. I couldn't imagine how long that would have taken.

It took ten seconds for the gates to open all the way. I tried to see inside, but there was just a lone orange light flickering weakly in the distance—and only darkness elsewhere.

"Huh...? I remember there being a huge hall here."

"We'll see when we get there. C'mon, let's go!" Asuna urged, tugging my arm. I hurried to keep up with her.

We stepped through the open gates and into the darkness. What little light there was from the bonfire shrooms covered the floor just past the gate, but nothing else could be seen.

For now, we could only head for the small light straight ahead... but that was probably just an ordinary fire. And if you stoked a fire, it would turn off all the bonfire shrooms through their chain reaction phenomenon.

But no sooner had I come to that conclusion than a number of needle-sharp spear points swung toward us from the darkness, prodding our chests.

I see. So that single flame was set on purpose, to keep all the mushrooms inside the hall dark...

My thought was snuffed out by a severe voice bellowing, "Human swordfighters Kirito and Asuna! You are under arrest for the crime of joining Kizmel the knight in stealing the sacred keys and passing them to the Fallen Elves!"

10

THE SOUND OF THE CELL CLOSING WAS SURPRISINGLY soft.

It wasn't due to the fact that the dark elf soldiers who took us to the cell were particularly gentlemanly. It was because the entire structure, as sturdy as it looked, was built of wood.

When the captain and his four soldiers left for the hallway and marched out of earshot, I took a look around the prison cell.

It was a small space, with two simple beds and one table. There was a pitcher of water and cups on the table. Instead of a lantern, a bonfire shroom glowed from a fixture on the wall.

I went over to the table and picked up the pitcher to examine it. The body was made of glass, but the handle was wood; the cups, meanwhile, were entirely wooden. The table and beds were constructed of complex tongue-and-groove joints, without a single visible nail. It seemed that the prison—and likely the entire palace—was made without any metal at all. The only exceptions were the weapons and armor the dark elves used.

Out of sheer habit, I lifted my hand to my left side, but there was no sword to touch. The Sword of Eventide, Asuna's Chivalric Rapier, and both of our Sigils of Lyusula had been confiscated when they took us here and put in a small storage room of some kind.

I stifled a sigh, grabbed a cup, and poured some water, sniffing it just in case before I drank it. No poison or paralysis debuff icons appeared, so I poured more water into the other cup and handed it to Asuna, who stood still in the center of the cell.

"Come on, drink up. It's just water."

"……Okay," she said, taking the cup with both hands and drinking it rather slowly. It wasn't very cold water, but it had the effect of calming her down a little; some light returned to her empty eyes. She blinked twice, then once more, and looked at me.

"…I wonder if Kizmel's being held in the cells here, too."

It was the question of the moment. I considered it briefly before replying, "If so, it's not anywhere near us. If she were close by, she'd have called for us already. Let's see…I wonder if it'll show up on the map…"

I opened my window and switched to the map tab. Fortunately, it displayed a map of Harin Tree Palace, so we examined it together. Most of it was still grayed out, but we could at least take a guess at the structure of the prison.

"This cell we're in now is on the west side of the second basement level. The stairs and the guard station are in the center. That tells me there's probably cells on the east side, too."

"And Kizmel is there?"

"It's possible," I said.

Asuna bit her lip. Eventually, through a voice hoarse with concealed pain, she said, "You remember what Kizmel said…when we asked her about having to take responsibility for losing the sacred keys on the sixth floor."

"Yeah…She said, '*I am one of the queen's own royal Pagoda Knights. Only Her Majesty and the knight commander have the right to formally rebook me…*' I mean, rebuke me."

"And like she said, I don't think Kizmel was punished in Castle Galey. If that were going to happen, she would've been put in the cells there. So…why did they lock her up here, on the seventh floor…?"

"Hmmm…"

Asuna's question was a good one. I stared up at the wood-paneled ceiling and mulled aloud, "If you interpret things as strictly as possible, that would mean that someone here at Harin Tree Palace has the authority to imprison Kizmel...either the commander of the Pagoda Knights or the dark elf queen herself. But I don't think that's actually possible. Those two don't leave their castle on the ninth floor. Which means...there's someone else here at this base that Kizmel doesn't know...someone with the same power as her commander?"

"Who would that be, for example?"

"For example, a different knights brigade, like...uhhh..."

When I got lost, Asuna was there to fill in the blanks in my memory.

"The Sandalwood Knights and Trifoliate Knights."

"Right, one of their commanders."

"But if the Pagoda Knights' commander doesn't leave the castle, wouldn't the same be true for the others?"

"...Good point," I had to admit. I hesitated, then added, "I'm going to spoil you a bit here...but when you get to the castle on the ninth floor, you end up taking some pretty long fetch quests for each of the three knight commanders. If any of them aren't present at the castle anymore, you wouldn't be able to take their quest or turn it in."

"I see..."

Asuna's brows creased, and she looked down, thinking hard. Then her head shot up.

"Oh...that's it! That's what we need to check! The quest log!"

"Oh."

I stared into her hazel-brown eyes, then quickly ran my finger along the open player window, switching from the map tab to the quest tab, then opening the "Elf War" campaign quest tree. There was a list of the completed quests from the previous floors—the "Jade Key," the "Lapis Key," the "Amber Key," the "Agate Key"— and then, at the bottom, a new title: the "Ruby Key."

I tapped the words to expand the tree further, bringing up the title of the first of the latest string of quests, presumably. It was "Prisoners of the Tree Palace."

Asuna and I put our heads together to read the tiny font on the quest log.

YOU HAVE BEEN SUSPECTED OF WORKING WITH THE FALLEN ELVES AND IMPRISONED IN THE CELLS OF HARIN TREE PALACE. TO CLEAR YOUR CHARGES, YOU MUST FIND A WAY TO REJOIN KIZMEL. START BY ESCAPING YOUR CELL AND RECOVERING YOUR CONFISCATED WEAPONS.

"…"

We were silent for three seconds, then we opened our mouths at the same time.

I made a *You first* gesture, so Asuna said quietly, "Does this mean that the Fallen Elves stealing the four keys was all part of the story? Or is this like what happened with Cylon…?"

"And someone—or something—has happened that was outside the expected bounds of the story line, so the quest has been altered to reflect that," I finished for her.

When the ax warrior Morte killed Cylon, the lord of Stachion on the sixth floor, I assumed it meant the "Curse of Stachion" quest was unfinishable. But the story absorbed the fact that another player had killed Cylon and guided us down a new path. The same thing was probably happening again here.

"…If so, we should probably assume that if the guards spot us escaping, they're not just going to put us back in here."

"That's true…It might even lead to them executing us. What should we do? Stay here and wait?"

"No," Asuna said at once. She stared at me with firm intent in her eyes. "The keys were stolen because Kizmel was trying to save us. If she's being tried for a crime because of that, we need to clear her charges and restore her honor at once."

"…Agreed," I said, closing my window. "So that means our first step is escape. Those bars are wood, from what I can tell, and I could probably break them with a sword skill from my sub-weapon, but it'll make a ton of noise…"

"Hmm…It would be one thing if we just had to run outside to freedom, but we need to get our weapons back and find Kizmel, too," Asuna grumbled. She walked up to the bars that separated the cell from the hallway.

I stood next to her, looking thoroughly. The wooden bars, with eyes and wood grain and all, were not rounded but rectangular. It was much like the prison bars in classic Japanese samurai movies. Each side was about an inch across, and they were placed at intervals of about six inches, vertically and horizontally. Even the Rat couldn't get through these bars.

That idea brought me back to our other duty. We were supposed to be gathering twenty ripe narsos fruits and delivering them to Nirrnir's room in Volupta by noon—or one o'clock at the latest.

The time was 5:40 AM. There was still lots of time, but at this point, Asuna's idea to leave three hours early was a brilliant one. In order to make use of this good fortune, we needed to meet up with Kizmel as quickly as possible and escape Harin Tree Palace.

I gripped one of the shining wooden bars and squeezed hard. I believed that my strength stat was among the higher levels in the frontline group, but this bar wasn't even creaking, much less breaking in half.

Next, I pulled a knife out of my inventory to see if I could cut the wood. But it was as though the bar had been finished with some kind of oil. The blade just slipped off the surface and couldn't find purchase.

I was thinking that it might be impossible to break the bars without making noise, when Asuna came over to me after examining the lock part of the door.

"I don't think we can get out with the Lock-picking skill."

"That figures...but we don't have time to put that into one of our slots and level it up from nothing..."

"I'm thinking that the wood material is the key to this. You don't have a saw, do you?"

"I do not...If I'd known it was going to come to this, I would've made off with one of that old shipbuilder's saws from the fourth floor."

"Or bought it, like a normal person," Asuna said, side-eyeing me. She traced the cornered wood with her finger. "I suppose... we could get a rat to chew through it..."

She was referring to a real rat, not Argo, of course. But the cell was clean, and I didn't see any holes in the baseboard where a family of rodents might be living.

"Or maybe...dump water on it and soften it up..."

We did have plenty of water, but it would probably take an entire month to rot away the wood enough to break it apart.

I scolded myself for only cutting down Asuna's ideas and not coming up with any of my own. But no matter how hard I thought, I wasn't reaching any brilliant conclusions. I was starting to think of desperate gambles like setting fire to the cage and using a sword skill in the chaos that ensued...when an idea arrived fully formed.

"...Fire," I muttered.

Asuna looked at me in surprise. "Fire...? You're going to start a fire in here?"

"No, not to burn the bars. To char them. If we cook them from a proper distance, it should drastically reduce their structural strength."

"But...it can't just be one spot. If we want to make a hole large enough for us to crawl through, we'll need to burn at least ten different spots on the bars..."

"Nope. Just one."

I pressed Asuna to move her out of the way, then stood in front of the door. It was also made of the same series of bars, except for the lock, which was enclosed inside a sturdy-looking box. And the mechanisms inside were probably—no, definitely—made of wood, too. If we toasted it for long enough from the outside, it should carbonize the insides.

Asuna's face lit up with surprise, and I opened my inventory to remove a torch. I was just about to light it when I realized something very important.

"Oh..."

"Wh-what's wrong?"

"Dammit! If we light it here, all the bonfire shrooms in the prison are going to go out in a chain reaction. If the shrooms in the guard station go out, too, they'll know we're using fire…"

I was so disappointed that I nearly threw the torch on the floor, but Asuna gripped my arm. "It's too early to give up. All we have to do is put out the fire before the chain reaction gets to the guard station, right?"

"Well…technically…"

"I'll watch the shrooms in the hallway from here. When I give the signal, put out the fire immediately."

"……"

It was a real tightrope act. But it didn't feel like we'd come up with a better plan or have the time to try.

"Fine…Uhhh…"

I pressed my face to the bars and looked down the hallway. There were bonfire shroom candlesticks on the walls between the cells, a line of green light that extended to the center of the second basement level, where the guard station would be.

"Let's say the one closest to us is number one. Tell me when… two, three, four, five…six of them go out."

"Got it. I'll tap your shoulder," said my partner. With the plan set, I crouched in front of the lock.

Taking up one square of the bar pattern—meaning a space six inches to a side—was a box containing a lock intricate enough that even dexterous Asuna would give up trying to solve it. But to be that delicate, it had to have low durability. I checked one more time to see that no one was patrolling the hallway, then tapped the torch and hit the IGNITE button.

A second after the orange flames appeared, the bonfire shroom lighting up the cell went out. Next, the mushrooms lining the hallway would go out. Keeping my panic in check, I lowered the flames toward the lock. The dark-brown wood did not change in any way at first, but eventually its surface got a little bit darker, and a tendril of smoke rose from it.

I felt a smack on my shoulder, and I quickly pressed the EXTIN-GUISH button on the pop-up window, which I'd left open for this purpose.

The torch instantly went out, plunging the cell into darkness. I waited, holding my breath, until the bonfire shroom on the wall behind us began to glow again. Every few seconds, one of the lights in the darkened hallway came back on.

"…Did that timing seem like it worked?" I whispered.

After a moment, Asuna replied, "Yes, I don't hear anyone coming from the station. I just realized, though…if there were any prisoners in the other cells around us, they would have made some noise…"

"True…Well, I guess that means it worked. Let's try it again. Keep watch!"

"On it."

Asuna took her position again, and I lit the torch. Each round of this gave me about ten seconds of time. Considering the possibility that soldiers might be patrolling the hallways in addition to waiting in the station, we couldn't take too long at this. I had to judge the exact effective distance that wouldn't light the lock on fire but would still carbonize it as quickly as possible.

The second heating burned the center of the wooden plate black. The third turned it red and heated, and the fourth caused cracks to spiral outward. In the real world, it would probably take significantly more powerful flames a longer amount of time to have the same effect, but dried wood in Aincrad was especially susceptible to fire.

On the fifth attempt, I nearly set it on fire and quickly batted it out with my bare hand. It felt hot, and it took a tiny bit of HP, but that didn't matter. Asuna focused on her watch and was considerate enough not to say anything.

On the sixth attempt, the center of the wooden plate turned to ash and crumbled, revealing the gears and deadbolt inside. As I suspected, they were all made of wood. The craftsmanship was extremely fine—it was a work of art. With a silent apology to the dark elf master who created it, I brought the flames close for a seventh time.

A number of gears carbonized before my eyes and crumbled away, followed by some faint sounds from the deadbolt attached to the doorframe as it came loose from the contraption. I put out the torch at once and got to my feet.

"It's open!"

"GJ!" Asuna said in a rare instance of gamer lingo, and we did a quick fist bump. I pushed the door gently, and it briefly pushed back but then came loose as flecks of charred wood were scraped free. Once we were sure there was no one in the corridor in either direction, we snuck out of the cell.

"First things first, we need to get our weapons," I murmured.

Asuna looked worried. "The room where they took our swords was next to the guard station. Can we even get inside without them noticing?"

"It'll be devastating if the room is locked. Still, we just have to figure it out."

"True."

We stopped talking and snuck along the hallway, checking at each set of cells on either side to ensure they were empty before proceeding. After we moved about sixty feet forward, a rectangular hall came into view ahead. That was the center of the second basement level. There was supposed to be an ascending staircase on the south side of it, with the guard station and storeroom side by side on the north end. We kept moving, even more carefully this time, until we could look around the corner of the hallway toward the station.

Just as I remembered, there were two doors side by side on the wall. Near the left door was a barred window. Bonfire shroom light much brighter than in the cells shone through it, accompanied by voices.

I made eye contact with Asuna, then crossed the hall in a crouch, until I was pressed against the wall just under the window. The volume of the voices increased, so that I could make out what they were saying.

"…sn't been a new prisoner in those cells in thirty years."

"And humankind, no less."

"They were fools for helping the Fallen."

"I presume they offered longer life, like usual."

"Humans always fall for that one."

Asuna's nostrils flared with indignation. I felt the same way, but it was imperative that we stay calm and careful right then.

Based on the voices, there were two guards in the station now. There were occasional sounds of tableware clattering, so they were probably eating breakfast. They didn't seem likely to leave the room for a little while.

We left the window and headed over to the door of the adjacent storage room. Praying that it wasn't locked, I examined the door—no lock at all. I quickly held the handle down, then pushed very slowly so as not to make any noise, and slipped inside through the crack.

As soon as Asuna was inside, I closed the door, and we shared a sigh of relief.

The dividing wall seemed thin, because we could still faintly hear the guards talking. We couldn't hold a normal conversation in here.

I gestured and said "Let's look for the weapons," then stood up to look around the storeroom. It was about the size of the cells, with three walls taken up by shelves and stands for swords and armor.

There were tons of wooden boxes and leather gloves and such stacked up on the shelves, and there were swords of all sizes stuck into the holders. If not for the situation, I would be jumping for joy, thinking it was a mountain of treasure, but the priority now was to recover our swords—and hopefully the rings, too.

I started by examining one of the sword stands, which was built much the same way as an umbrella holder from the real world. All the swords jammed into it were on the verge of falling apart, as though they'd been there for decades. If I treated them too roughly, I could easily knock off their hilts and knuckle guards.

For a minute or so, I picked through them with my finger-tips. Annoyingly, I finally found some sheaths with a familiar color and shape, all the way in the back, as though they had been placed there as a prank. Still, this was a relief.

Not far away, Asuna waved to say *Found it!* But she was pointing at a different sword stand, of course.

I pulled the Sword of Eventide and Chivalric Rapier free, then looked over to where Asuna was pointing. It was a longsword with details that were slightly different from the usual dark elven make, along with a saber in a black-leather sheath.

That settled it. The longsword was the Elven Stout Sword we'd taken from the forest elf captain. And the saber was Kizmel's weapon, which had been snapped by Kysarah, the Fallen Elf adjutant. We'd given Kizmel the forest elf sword to use after her saber was broken. That all but confirmed that Kizmel was somewhere in this prison.

I handed Asuna her rapier and mounted my sword on my back, then pulled the stout sword and saber out of the stand together. But something in my haste must have caused my hands to slip. An old-fashioned sword stuck in the same hole as those two wobbled and started to lean toward the adjacent hole.

Aaaaah!

I screamed silently. If the sword smacked against another, which pushed the next one, and so on, like a stack of dominoes, it would make a tremendous clatter. I wanted to grab the sword to stop it, but my hands were full. I'd have to stop it with my mouth or use psychic powers to keep it in place…

A hand shot forward and blocked it just in the nick of time. Asuna was leaning over as far as she possibly could, propping up the old sword by her fingertips. I started to relax with relief, but then it was Asuna who was losing her balance.

Oh, dear God! I prayed, sticking the arm holding Kizmel's saber under her body. I didn't have time to get the right spot, so it ended up taking the brunt of her chest. Through my arm, I felt the toughness of her breastplate—and the resiliency of what was behind it.

Much, much later, Asuna would wistfully say, *"If we hadn't been working together for a month already by that point, I would have tossed the swords and yelled my head off."*

Fortunately, Asuna's avatar simply went as stiff as a board. She did not yell or rage.

With my right arm, I pushed the Asuna statue upright, bit by bit. Then I took a step back, and we looked at each other.

"...This sword is really heavy," she murmured quietly. In her left hand was the aged sword that had nearly fallen.

"Hang on," I whispered back at the same volume, putting the stout sword and saber into my inventory. With my hand free, I accepted the sword from Asuna; it was indeed quite hefty, much more so than my Sword of Eventide.

There was a large knuckle guard attached to the hilt, and its white-leather sheath was slightly curved. This wasn't a longsword, but it was a saber like Kizmel's. The whole thing was dirty, and there was even a spiderweb on the inside of the guard, so it didn't look like a luxury item. Nevertheless, I put it into my inventory, too, just in case Kizmel found it easier to use.

That had been nerve-racking, but we completed our initial objective and got back our swords. Next up, I wanted the rings, but with the number of boxes and bags in the room, we'd need way more than just five or ten minutes. Of course, the purpose of the sigil was to allow you free entrance to any dark elf base, so the fact that we'd been arrested probably nullified that privilege.

I quietly explained as much to Asuna. She looked around the multiple stacked shelves at all the metal and wooden boxes—and leather and cloth bags.

"In that case," she whispered, "couldn't we just stick the boxes and bags into our inventories and look through them later? At least some of them, if not all."

"......"

Her bold idea left me speechless. Time-limited item searches were a common event in RPGs, but taking the containers

themselves out of the room *had* to be outside the bounds of the scenario writer's intention.

On the other hand, all those boxes weren't fixed to the shelf. If there was any worry, it was that taking them would be identified as theft and turn us into orange players, but if so, I should have received a warning at the point I put that antique saber into my item storage. We were outside the anti-criminal code area of town, so the only punishment we could suffer for stealing was through dark elf law, not the game system itself.

I reached out to the shelf and carefully lifted the wooden box that was placed on top of the pile of varied containers. There were no anti-theft alarms. The box was not especially heavy. I placed it atop the inventory window, and it vanished with a little flash of blue-light particles.

"……"

"……"

We shared a silent look, then began shoveling the boxes and bags into our inventory. Because our levels were significantly higher than the recommended number for this area, and the fact that we weren't carrying a bunch of heavy weapons around, we had plenty of space. By the time we had both reached 90 percent of our carrying capacity, the number of containers had dwindled to under a third. The Sigils of Lyusula might be in one of the containers we didn't grab, of course, but we didn't want to load up to the maximum, in case our weight limit was crossed at an inopportune time and left us immobilized.

When our box thievery was complete, I closed my window and concentrated on my ears. The guards in the station next door were still talking. Even in an underground prison, the dark elves' love of tea and chatter held true.

We opened the door again and headed into the open hall. On the wall opposite us was the stairway we'd been taken down less than an hour ago. On the right was the hallway leading to the cells on the west side. And as I expected (or hoped), there was a hallway leading to the east on the left. If Kizmel was a prisoner here, she would be that way.

I glanced at Asuna, then snuck down the eastern hallway.

Using the bonfire shroom light, we looked into each set of cells lining the corridor. The actual amount of light from the mushrooms was meager, but they stayed on, even in cells with no occupants, so a mere glance showed us the contents of each one as we passed.

But because of that, we rapidly ran lower and lower on cells to check. We were already halfway down the corridor and still hadn't seen Kizmel yet.

There were eight cells on either side of the sixty-foot hallway, sixteen in total. Eight cells left to check…seven, six, five. Each of them was empty—and didn't look like they'd been used in years, if not decades.

Our feet felt heavier and heavier as we neared the end. But we had to keep checking. Four more, three, two…

"…!!"

The instant we looked into the last cell, we both sucked in a sharp breath.

It took all of two seconds for our hopes to deflate. One of the two beds was occupied by a figure lying on its side, but the silhouette very obviously did not belong to Kizmel. The body was large for an elf and clearly male.

I held my gaze on him until a yellow cursor appeared. The name was DARK ELVEN PRISONER. That didn't tell us who it was, but if he wasn't Kizmel, we had no reason to talk to him. We'd just be ruining ourselves if he raised a fuss and brought the guards running.

I motioned for Asuna to back away, and I inched backward on my heels. The prisoner's back was toward us, so he wouldn't notice us unless we made noise.

Or so I thought. I hadn't moved more than a foot when the prisoner said quietly, "You're not elves. Who are you?"

We froze with shock, and the figure rose and turned to face us.

He was wearing a simple outfit of a cotton shirt and pants that had once been black but had faded to gray. His hair and beard had grown out to the point that I couldn't even discern his features. Behind his hanging black bangs, I could see gleaming, intense eyes.

"W-we're nobodies. We'll just be leaving," I managed to stammer, resuming my retreat.

"If you don't answer me, I'll call the guards," his rusty voice said, nailing me down on the spot.

"Umm…I'm the human swordsman Kirito, and this is Asuna."

"What are you doing here?"

"We're looking for someone…"

"Who?"

His questions were short and direct, leaving me no time to think about lying to him. I just had to steel myself and tell the truth.

"A knight by the name of Kizmel. She was brought here within the last day, we believe…"

"Kizmel…from what family?" he asked, to our surprise. I looked to Asuna, but the fencer just shook her head.

I turned back to him and said, "Uh, I don't know."

"Hmm…Then I don't know, either," said the prisoner, reaching for his side table and pouring water from the pitcher to his wooden cup; they were the same things we had in our cell. He finished the water in one gulp and set down the cup, then asked, "And you were the ones who were brought here a little while ago?"

"Y-yes."

"Then this knight Kizmel is not being held on this floor. I have been imprisoned here for thirty years, and you are the first prisoners since my arrival."

"Thirty years…" I repeated, stunned.

A month ago, I would have assumed this was just the background for his story. After all, in 1993, thirty years before 2023, there was no *SAO*. There wasn't even a single VRMMO with old-fashioned head-mounted displays.

But after meeting Kizmel and learning about the long history of war between the forest elves and the dark elves, my way of thinking had begun to change. If not for the human players diving into this server, they could run time in this world as fast as the server specs allowed, so it was possible that before *SAO* launched, they had compiled a history of the centuries since the Great Separation of Aincrad, if not even further into the past.

"Um...why are you in this cell?" asked Asuna over my shoulder, her voice hoarse.

The bearded man's eyes fixed on Asuna. "For no reason that you need to know, human girl."

He was lying on his side again, sending the message that our conversation was over.

But I persisted. I didn't want to leave without learning something useful.

"Um, are there other cells here in Harin Tree Palace?"

The man didn't say anything for several seconds, until at last I heard him snort. Something struck me as strange...but I couldn't hold on to the thought, because he started speaking into the mushroom-lit gloom.

"There is also a prison in the priests' living quarters on the seventh story. If the crime this Kizmel committed has to do with them, she may have been taken there."

"B-but...Kizmel's sword was in the storeroom down there..." I blurted out. The man rose up again.

"You got into the storeroom?"

"W-well, yes."

"Hmm...And how did you get out of your cell without the guards noticing?"

"Uh...I used a torch to burn the lock on the door..."

"......"

The man's broad shoulders trembled. A few moments later, I

heard him uttering short, quiet sounds and realized at last that he was laughing.

Please don't start screaming with laughter, I prayed. Fortunately, the chuckles got softer and softer until he was done. He shook his head, then said dryly, "I see...your human Art of Mystic Scribing. The guards certainly cannot inspect that."

"Uh, y-yeah..." I replied, my mind racing.

We could use the same method to break the lock on this man's cell, too. Following quest logic, if we freed this man, he would presumably help us. Assuming this story development was written by someone employed by Argus, that would be the proper answer.

But more than likely, our trip through the "Elf War" campaign questline was far off the track of its original scenario. Now that Akihiko Kayaba had turned *SAO* into what it was, and Argus was no longer managing the game, it was impossible to imagine a flesh-and-blood person carefully modifying quests for every living player. And if the game system itself was rewriting the quest in real time, I had to assume that the typical expectations were out the window.

This prisoner was a living human being—er, dark elf. Could he be trusted or not? That was the real question.

A thirty-year sentence in this underground prison meant he must have committed quite a crime. So what was it? He'd just said, "Nothing you need to know about, human." So maybe there was another clue...

"Um, do you have any brothers?" Asuna asked out of the blue. I turned to look at her, stunned.

The man was surprised, too, it seemed. He blinked in silence, then replied, "What made you ask that?"

"Because I know a dark elf who looks very similar to you."

In my head, I was thinking *Whaaaaat?* If Asuna knew him, then I knew him, too, presumably. But what dark elf did I know who looked like this prisoner with scraggly hair and a grown-out beard...? And speaking of male dark elves, the only ones I really "knew" to any extent were Viscount Leyshren Zed Yofilis at Yofel Castle, old Bouhroum at Castle Galey, and maybe Count Melan Gus Galeyon. The only thing any of them shared in common with this man was the color of their skin…

I felt another crackle of electricity run through the center of my brain. My eyes shot open.

No. There was another dark elf I knew—if you could use that verb.

Asuna waited until she was certain I'd figured it out, too. "He did not tell us his name, but he works as a blacksmith in a camp on the third floor. He strengthened this sword of mine."

She walked closer to the cell, squeezing the grip of the Chivalric Rapier. She pulled it out of the sheath backhanded, then extended the pommel through the bars.

I would have taken several seconds to mull this one over before I acted. But there wasn't a single ounce of hesitation in Asuna's expression.

The prisoner stared at us through his long bangs, then abruptly stepped out of the bed. He stuck his feet into sandals that were barely more than scraps of material, then walked up to the bars. He grabbed the hilt of the rapier Asuna was holding toward him and pulled it into the cell.

He held it up near his forehead, allowing the light from the bonfire shroom on the wall behind him to illuminate the shining blade, then said, "Yes, I can see that Landeren tempered this sword. He produced nothing but junk before…but after thirty years, I suppose the bungler has learned a few things."

Assuming Landeren was the name of that exceedingly unfriendly blacksmith, I was afraid to even imagine how he would react to being called a bungler. At the very least, I knew he'd do more than snort…and *that* was when I realized what had been setting off my déjà vu earlier. The way he exhaled through his nose was exactly the same as how the blacksmith had.

The man spun the rapier around, then stuck the hilt back through the bars. Asuna grabbed it, then took a step back.

"If you've done a service for my brother, then I should thank you. I will help you search for Kizmel the knight."

I didn't even have time to marvel over this sudden change in attitude when Asuna pointed out, "That's very kind of you, but he was the one who did a service for *us*..."

"An elf blacksmith will only see the chance to work on a sword that fine a number of times in his life. I'm certain that the experience will have helped my little brother grow."

"Are you a blacksmith, too?"

"......No," the prisoner said, the bangs that hung to his nose swaying. "I did not have the talent. My brother had the blacksmith's blood in his veins, like my father and grandfather...but I did not even have that..."

He stopped there, returning to the bed. I started to worry that he'd changed his mind about helping us, but instead of rolling back onto the mattress, he grabbed the faded sheet and carefully tore a strip from the corner. Then he used the makeshift rope to tie his long hair behind his head.

Revealed at last, the man's face had all the sternness of a typical dark elf, despite his overgrown facial hair. By human years, he looked like he was in his late thirties. He was indeed quite similar to the blacksmith on the third floor—but there was one other feature that caused me to gasp.

Running across his face from cheek to cheek, about an inch under his eyes, was a sword scar. It was not a new wound, but it stood out starkly against his dark skin. It must have been quite deep when it was inflicted.

Sensing our eyes, the man ran his thumb along the mark and snorted. He strode up to the bars and eyed the direction of the guard station. Asuna and I glanced down the hallway. There was no sign of the guards leaving the room yet, but they would probably come patrolling once their meal was over. My intuition told me we had a few minutes at most.

"I'm going to burn the lock. Step back, please," I said, but the man shook his head.

"Do not bother. Instead, go to the storeroom next to the station and bring back my sword."

Really? You want us to search through all those swords?! I thought, keeping it to myself. "What…kind of sword is it?"

"A saber. Its hilt and guard are silver, while the handle and sheath are white leather. You might not recognize it by those details, because it's surely covered in thirty years of dust…"

""……""

Asuna and I stared at each other.

I opened my inventory, sorted weapons by *most recent*, then tapped the first name on the list, the Saber of Santalum Knights, and materialized it.

The large saber appeared with a soft sound. I used both hands to lift it up.

Dirtiness effects were supposed to disappear after a short period of time in this world, but the grime fixed to the hilt and the spiderweb inside the knuckle guard were as I recognized them earlier. They would probably clean up some if I used a cloth, but it seemed like a strange thing to do, so I stuck the handle through the bars.

The man hesitated for just an instant, then grabbed the saber and pulled it through to the cell, sheath and all.

When he noticed the spiderweb, he snorted, then grabbed his bedsheet again and quickly but carefully rubbed the entire saber with it. It regained its sheen and looked good as new—or at least, not quite as old. He stuck the sheath onto his belt on the left side, then drew the weapon.

The finely curved blade gave off a dull shine in the light of the bonfire shrooms. That wasn't because of any grime on the weapon, though. It was the quality of a fine weapon, one that had seen many years of combat and upkeep. My Anneal Blade +8, which had broken in the battle against the forest elf knight, had the same sheen to it.

I thought back to my old trusty weapon, which still slumbered in the depths of my inventory in its broken state. The man glared at me and warned, "Step back."

"Ah, r-right."

Asuna and I backed away from the bars. The man moved to the door, then held the naked saber overhead.

I didn't even have time to cry *Whoa, wait!* The blade took on a silver shine, then rang like a piece of struck glass. It was the warm-up effect of a sword skill.

If he knocked down the door with sheer strength, it would make an incredible racket and bring the guards down on us immediately. After all the trouble we'd gone to silently carbonizing the lock, this was going to ruin everything.

A silver light flickered in the darkness. Two or three tiny sparks appeared in the gap between the door and the next bar.

That was it. No deafening crash, not even as much sound as a cup being placed on the table. The saber was back to its spot over the man's head, which made me wonder if he'd even used the sword skill at all. But there was no denying the perfectly vertical silver line he'd created.

He returned the saber to its sheath, stepped forward, and pushed the door with his thumb. It made the slightest of creaks and swung open, easy as that. The part of the lock bolt left on the door was cut through so cleanly that it looked like it had been polished that way.

"...Wh-what was that technique?" I asked without thinking.

The man shrugged and said, "It is called Slashing Ray...I believe."

I'd never heard of that skill. Most likely, it was an elite skill in the Curved Blade category. I was tempted to ask to see his stats, but I didn't even know how to open up an NPC's status window. Maybe if you tapped on their hair whorl, it would open a properties window. I certainly didn't have the courage to attempt that with this old ma...er, young man.

The man exited the cell into the hallway, then stretched and cracked his neck from side to side. If he'd really been trapped in that cell for thirty straight years, then he had to be experiencing a bewildering sense of freedom, but a few mere stretches and cracks had him satisfied, apparently. His steel-gray eyes fixed the two of us with a glare.

"What did you say your names were?"

"Uh, I'm Kirito…"

"And I'm Asuna."

The man repeated, "Kirito and Asuna." His pronunciation was perfect, and of all the NPCs we'd met, his check was the shortest. We confirmed that he was right, and then he said, "I am Lavik."

That was the indication that he was joining the party. A new HP bar appeared underneath ours in the upper left of my view.

It also showed me the name that had been on his cursor. It went from DARK ELVEN PRISONER to LAVIK, DARK ELVEN FUGITIVE. The English word *fugitive* did not have an entry in my mental dictionary, but I could ask Asuna later. First, I asked Lavik which way we were going now.

"So…how do we get up to the seventh story to find Kizmel?"

"She *might* be on the seventh story," Lavik corrected brusquely. "First, we need to get information from the guards."

"Huh?! A…are you going to bribe them?"

"Only if you have enough money to buy a lakeside mansion on the ninth floor."

We shook our heads. The bearded dark elf snorted yet again.

"Then we'll use swords."

11

IT WAS SEVEN O'CLOCK, ONE HOUR AFTER WE'D escaped from our cell.

I was hanging off a nearly sheer cliff by a lifeline less than a fraction of an inch wide, desperately trying to descend the outer wall of Harin Tree Palace.

It was a natural tree trunk, not an artificial wall, so at least there were little outcroppings of bark I could rest my hands and feet on, but it was still a hundred and fifty feet down to the ground. If I slipped, and the tiny rope failed to support my weight, the fall damage alone would take out all my HP.

But I couldn't whine and give up now. Just three feet to my left, Asuna was silently descending the wall with another rope tied around her sword belt, and on my right, Lavik was going straight down like an experienced rock climber.

But worst of all was the dark elf knight who'd just joined the party a few minutes ago, looking up at me with concern from my left.

"Are you all right, Kirito?" she wondered.

I did my very best to put on what I hoped resembled a smile and said, "I'm f-fine! Don't worry about me; just keep going."

"You know I can't do that. I told you, if your foot slips, I'll be there to keep you up," Kizmel reassured me.

When we'd rescued her from the cells on the seventh story of the palace, she had been quite haggard. Fortunately, she hadn't suffered any physical damage and still had all her equipment aside from her weapons, but it was clear that being accused of treachery with the Fallen Elves and then imprisoned was an unbearable humiliation for such a proud knight.

She had been overjoyed to see us, of course, but it was so bad that she initially refused to escape the prison. With enough convincing from Asuna and me (and Lavik), Kizmel had made up her mind to clear her reputation herself and escaped out the seventh-story window with us—which was why we were here now.

I listened carefully and heard the shouts of guards within the palace, as well as footsteps rushing in every direction. It was going to take a while for that confusion to resolve. That was because of Asuna's clever idea: leaving the lit torch in a small side room in a corner of the seventh story.

The chain reaction from the flames caused every last bonfire shroom in Harin Tree Palace to extinguish itself. Until they found and put out the torch, the entire palace was trapped in darkness. That wasn't conducive to running an intensive search. We needed to escape into Looserock Forest while they were still in a panic.

I banished the hundred-plus-foot drop below my feet from my mind and focused on nothing but the trunk. I put a hand on a small hole, then my foot on a protruding knot, then grabbed a hanging vine and stepped on a chunk of broken bark. In an old-school RPG, I'd be able to just hold the controller stick down to effortlessly zip down the surface. But the immersive nature of a full-dive VRMMO was what made it function so effectively as a game of life and death. If I found a little extra time, I needed to practice my climbing, just in case I got myself into a situation like this again. If I got good enough to scurry up and down the pillars along the outer aperture of Aincrad, I wouldn't be afraid of any cliff again…

These thoughts kept my mind occupied while I climbed down the tree. But engaging in an escape from reality to forget my fear began to sap my concentration as well. I thought my toe was firmly on a knot, but it slipped off, causing my stomach to lurch up into my throat.

Fortunately, my foot merely dropped a few inches before landing on a hard, flat surface.

I looked down and saw that it was resting on a stone pillar about three feet across. Somehow, I had reached the rock surface that surrounded the palace. I looked around and saw Asuna, Lavik, and Kizmel staring back at me, having finished their descent already.

I cleared my throat awkwardly, then undid the lifeline tied to my sword belt. The rope was one we'd found in a storeroom on the seventh story and was so fine and powerful that it couldn't be cut unless you sawed at it repeatedly with a steel blade. It felt bad to leave it behind, but the other end was tied around a thick branch a hundred and fifty feet overhead, so there was no way to get it down.

I trotted down the staircase-like pillars in order, until I reached the corridor where the other three were waiting for me.

"Here I am," I said as breezily as possible, and Kizmel smiled and said, "You did well, Kirito."

It was hard not to feel like a child who had just climbed down from the top of the jungle gym all on his own.

We avoided the southern direction, where the main gate to the palace was located, and instead entered the west passageway, which was closest to where we descended the tree. We made our way across the bridge of loose rocks, checking to make sure they weren't pursuing us. None of us fell into the water on the trip back to the entrance.

All we had to do was pass through the tunnel entryway to the forest, and we'd be outside—but there was something to take care of first.

I glanced back in the direction of the palace, then said to Kizmel, "Um…I know it's an emergency situation, but do you mind if we take a detour?"

"A detour? But there is nothing but marshland around here."

"We need something called narsos fruit that grows here..."

"Really? You humans have excellent taste," said not Kizmel, but Lavik. He scratched at his wild beard and smirked. "It's a kick and a tingle on the tongue, but once you get used to them, you'll love the thrill of it. I haven't had one in ages."

I didn't have time to correct him that we weren't *eating* the fruit before Kizmel replied, "Hmm...I'm not the biggest admirer of narsos..."

She was grimacing as though she'd bitten into a sour persimmon.

Lavik smacked her bracingly on the back. "Don't complain, Kizmel! Narsos is good for the body and spirit. You could use some of that right now."

"But, Sir Lavik, the swamp has those detestable leeches in it."

"Hrm...the hematomelibe? Yes, those are a pain...They'll stay away if you drip some mint oil into the water. Does anyone have some?" Lavik asked, looking to us, but we just shook our heads. I didn't know every last item in my inventory in minute detail, but I certainly couldn't recall picking up any mint oil.

"That's too bad...Well, they're a necessity for any soldiers patrolling Looserock Forest, so they should have stockpiles of them here and there around the palace. How about we turn around, go back, and get some?"

"Lavik, I don't think that will be necessary," said Kizmel, looking partially annoyed and partially worried. But the suggestion put an idea into my mind, and I opened my inventory.

If it was true that they kept bits of it here and there around the palace, then perhaps there was a bottle in that underground storage room, too. And if that bottle happened to be in one of the boxes that Asuna and I took from there...

She was on the same track that I was. She opened her window and tapped on the item names from the top—AGED WOODEN BOX, RUSTY IRON BOX, BOILED LEATHER SACK, LINEN SACK, and so on—to peruse their contents.

Most of it was worthless junk, and while there were a few

interesting pieces, like necklaces and charms and keys, I put off identifying any of them, focusing purely on the four letters *m-i-n-t*.

After tapping through at least a dozen boxes and scrolling through the list of their contents, I was heading for another one when I gasped, "Ah!"

I scrolled back up the list I'd just been about to close. Sitting right in the middle, plain as day, was the name Sigil of Lyusula. And there were two of them.

I was quickly taking them out when Asuna also gasped. There was a rapid materialization sound effect after that, and I saw a small green bottle resting atop her menu window. She looked at mine and again exclaimed, "Ah!"

I was going to give one of the rings to Asuna, but I stopped. They were both identical in design, with the symbol of Lyusula carved on them. Of course, they didn't have our names on them, so at a glance, there was no way to tell which was Asuna's and which was mine.

Racked with indecision, I was merely pinching my thumb and index finger back and forth, so Asuna thrust out her hand. "It doesn't matter which is which. They're both the same," she snapped.

That was true, of course. Equipment items in *SAO* were automatically adjusted to the size of the wielder, so the original size did not matter. I picked up one and stuck it on the index finger of Asuna's outstretched hand. For some reason, she twitched and arched her back but failed to say anything. I put the other ring on my own hand, then snatched the bottle off the top of Asuna's window.

"Found some mint oil," I told Lavik, who was surveying the spacious swamp, and held out the bottle.

The whiskered swordsman's face broke into a smile. "Ah, that is good. Then let us search for that narsos," he said, taking the bottle. "And don't worry. Even if the hematomelibe do bite, you just have to put up with it and wait, and they'll drift off somewhere else."

Kizmel made a face of disgust like I'd never seen before. Having said almost the exact same thing to Asuna, I could only smile awkwardly and give him a little nod in response.

Apparently, Lavik had a preternatural ability to sniff out the scent of narsos fruit, because it took barely three minutes in the marshland for him to find the tree we were looking for.

The mint oil lived up to its reputation, too. A single drop of it into the water every thirty seconds really did keep the bloodsucking slugs away from us. Argo wouldn't know about this, either, but Looserock Forest was almost an entirely pointless location if you weren't playing the dark elf side of the campaign quest. Now that Qusack, the quest-focused guild we met on the sixth floor, had retreated from the front line, there wouldn't be any players coming here for a while yet.

The narsos tree, which was growing in a nondescript area of the wetland, looked very similar to a willow from the real world, except that hanging from the end of its long, delicate branches right near the water was a fruit shaped like a mango. If it were yellow like a mango, I might have been tempted to take a bite, but instead it was covered in eye-melting stripes of alternating reddish-purple and light green. It was clearly a warning signal.

Asuna and Kizmel were just as hesitant as I was, but Lavik was delighted at his discovery and sloshed over to lift one of the branches, pulling off one of the bulging fruits. He smelled it reverently, breathing deep, then took a big bite.

After the pleasant crunch of the bite, my sinuses became filled with a complex smell that was both sweet and spicy. I imagined Lavik grunting and collapsing, but the swordsman simply continued to chew happily.

Suddenly, an icon that looked like the narsos fruit appeared over Lavik's HP bar. I couldn't tell from the look of it whether it was a buff or debuff. According to Nirrnir, this fruit was the base ingredient for the dye-removing bleach, but I didn't see his black hair turning white or anything. It was all rather confusing.

The swordsman pulled off another fruit while he ate and offered it to me. "There are plenty on the tree. Don't be shy; have some, Kirito."

I wasn't being shy; trust me, I thought.

But out loud, I gave him a timid "Th-thank you" and glanced at the narsos tree. There were at least fifty fruits at a glance, so eating one or two wouldn't affect the twenty we needed for the quest. I rubbed it with the sleeve of my shirt, then hesitantly sank my teeth into it.

The texture was not like a mango, but a pear, yet the scent reminded me of lychee and pepper. The skin was thin, and the flesh was juicy, with plenty of sweetness. If anything, it was one of the better fruits I'd eaten in Aincrad...

Until a sudden, startling electric shock ran through my tongue.

"Hurrgh!" I yelped, feeling rather pathetic. Lavik laughed uproariously. He was certainly much more sociable than his little brother, Landeren. What crime could he have committed to be sentenced to prison for thirty years?

I waited patiently for the buzzing numbness on my tongue to subside and saw the flashy icon appear on my HP bar, too. The effects weren't clear from here, but there was a way to find out.

I quickly opened my window and went to the status tab. The same icon was there, so I tapped it with my finger. It said: NAR-SOS STIMULATION: SLIGHT INCREASE TO PARALYSIS AND STUN RESISTANCE.

I couldn't help but think, *Not worth it!*

But I couldn't just throw out the remainder or foist it off on Asuna, so I steeled myself and devoured the rest as quickly as I could. Fortunately, the shock effect did not last while the buff was active, so I was able to eat it just fine, to my relief.

On the other side of the tree, Asuna and Kizmel were quickly harvesting the fruits. Their faces were a rictus of determination *not* to take a bite of any of them.

I joined them, thinking of how I might slip a piece onto Asuna's plate during a meal someday. Lavik claimed the ones that grew lower to the ground were riper, so I picked from the bottom up. Asuna took fifteen, and I took ten, with the extras being just in case. A quest update message appeared briefly.

That finished our duty in Looserock Forest. Lavik asked for a container to hold the fruits, so I picked out one of the cloth bags from my inventory and gave it to him, which he stuffed with close to ten more fruits. If he really enjoyed the electric sensation of the fruits, he was probably just a different type of person from the rest of us.

We returned to the western end of the green corridor, dripping mint oil along the way, and climbed the rock staircase there. Once through the tunnel of trees, we saw white light ahead.

The four of us walked faster and faster, until we were practically racing out of the tunnel and into the morning light over the meadows.

Many low hills rose in succession, covered in deep green. Beyond them, shrouded in gray, was a massive structure—the labyrinth tower of the seventh floor, connecting the ground to the bottom of the floor above us.

It had been chilly in the forest, but the temperature was already much higher outside. A gentle southern breeze sent waves rustling through the grass, carrying the fragrance of flowers.

We walked forward about twenty meters into the meadow and up a hill, then turned back.

The forest rose like a mountain of its own, the tightly packed branches rustling. From the outside, you could never imagine the fantastical glowing tunnels of greenery and majestic palace built into the giant tree that lay under that canopy. From here it was already nearly impossible to see the entrance to the tunnel we'd just come through.

Once we had waited and listened, certain there were no pursuers coming after us, the group stretched and relaxed.

"Mmm…so this is what color the sunlight was," Lavik grunted, squinting and blinking. It occurred to me that he hadn't seen any light other than the green of the bonfire shrooms for over three decades.

The former prisoner's grown-out beard and tied-up hair waved in the southern breeze. Kizmel addressed him formally.

"...Sir Lavik, allow me to thank you again. I would have been tried by the priests for a crime I did not commit and, most likely, never given the chance to leave prison and restore my honor," she said, bowing deeply.

Lavik's voice took on a sterner complexion. "It is too early to thank me, knight. Now you are not a prisoner, but a fugitive. It may be ironic of me to say this, given that I urged you to escape, but if they capture you again before you clear your charges, they will do more than simply imprison you. The real struggle begins now."

"Yes, I understand that very well. The Fallen Elves stole the four sacred keys because of my failure and lack of strength. I must forge myself anew and succeed this time..."

"Not so fast," Lavik said, holding up a hand to stop her. He glanced at Asuna and me, then asked the knight, "What was the name of the Fallen who defeated you, Kirito and Asuna?"

"...Kysarah the Ransacker."

"*Her*...In that case, you cannot be blamed for losing. There is no dark elf *or* forest elf alive who can defeat Kysarah in single combat or even force a draw."

"But—!" Kizmel protested, stepping forward with a clank of armor.

Lavik continued, "If the legend that gave her the epithet of Ransacker is true, then her strength comes from ransacking the Holy Tree itself, a cursed power from stripping its bark and severing its branches. Meanwhile, the people of Lyusula have long suffered from the loss of the Holy Tree's blessing...If you wish to gain power equal to Kysarah's, ordinary training will not suffice."

"Then, Sir Lavik, must I tuck my tail between my legs and run every time Kysarah appears?!"

"I did not say that." Lavik shook his head, then glanced our way and continued, "Kizmel the knight. You have already gained a power that no people of Lyusula or Kales'Oh have ever possessed."

"Wh-what is that…?"

"Your way with humankind…Your bond."

Asuna and I held our breath. Lavik gazed up at the bottom of the floor above, the surface faded and blue with distance. His voice was tinged with a faint sense of sadness and longing.

"Even before our bondage in this floating castle, we elves have long been separate from the other races, seeing them as our inferiors. Humankind, dwarfkind, fairies like the villi and sylphs…But the people of the other races have their own strength that others do not share. And I am not speaking of the Arts of Mystic or Far Scribing. I speak of…"

He stopped there, reached out, and patted Kizmel on the left shoulder. Then he approached and did the same to the two of us.

"You already know what I wish to say. Follow your heart's guidance, and you will gain the power to break Kysarah…to break General N'ltzahh himself."

No way, no way, no way! I nearly screamed.

Fortunately, I held it in. If we continued this questline, we would eventually have to fight the general, he of the pitch-black color cursor. And after how far we'd come, there was simply no option for Asuna and me to abandon Kizmel and continue our quest through Aincrad without completing her mission.

Lavik gave us a smile, crinkling his long sword scar, and turned around. Over his shoulder, he said gently, "You have done me a great favor, Kirito and Asuna. Take good care of Kizmel."

He began walking to the north, but Asuna called out, "Um! Do you think…just for a little bit, while we're on this floor…you could…"

But Lavik did not stop.

He raised his hand and waved it briefly, continuing on his way. All he had were his worn-out prisoner's clothes and sandals, the saber at his side, and the narsos fruit in the sack for food.

I couldn't begin to guess where he was going to go, dressed like that.

Lavik's figure descended the hill, until he was lost in the sea of grass. Moments later, his HP bar vanished from our party list.

The only thing present was the sound of the wind, until Kizmel finally spoke.

"I believe that man was the previous commander of the Sandalwood Knights Brigade, Lavik Fen Cortassios."

""*Commander*?!"" Asuna and I yelped together.

The Sandalwood Knights were one of the three brigades of Lyusula. Between the way he sliced through the lock on the cell without a sound and knocked out the two guards with a single strike with the back of his sword, we could tell he was quite a warrior—but *that* important?

"Wh-why would he have been in prison for thirty years...?" I squawked, stunned.

Kizmel just shook her head. "I do not know the precise reason; it is not a matter of official record. However...from the rumors I heard, it may have had something to do with Viscount Yofilis..."

""Huh?!"" we yelped together again.

I was shocked, but Asuna quickly recovered and seemed to have put it together.

"Ohhh...Lavik's younger brother called Viscount Yofilis Leyshren, remember? If the younger brother, Landeren, was friendly with the viscount, then maybe the elder...brother..."

Her words slowed down awkwardly, and I thought I knew why.

Viscount Leyshren Zed Yofilis was the master of Yofel Castle on the fourth floor, and on his face was a vertical scar that traveled from his forehead and through his left eye to his chin.

And on former Commander Lavik's face was a similarly deep scar that ran left to right.

Asuna and I looked to Kizmel for answers. But the knight just shook her head.

"...It is not for me to say what Viscount Yofilis did not tell you himself. I suspect Sir Lavik will use a spirit tree to go to the fourth…"

She let that statement trail off, too, then exhaled and changed gears.

Kizmel walked right toward us, arms outstretched, and enveloped Asuna in a tight hug.

"Thank you, Asuna," she whispered, her voice thick with emotion. Then she turned to me. Smiling, she circled her arms around my back and squeezed with enough force that my breastplate creaked.

It wasn't the first time I hugged Kizmel, but the awkwardness was still there, I realized. Thankfully, this time the majority of what I felt was relief and gratitude at our reunion.

"Thank you, Kirito," she whispered into my ear, and I hugged her back. There was heat in the corner of my eyes, but for some reason, this was the moment the quest log chose to intrude with an update message, which pulled me back to more immediate concerns.

Naturally, our reunion with Kizmel did not mean our problems were solved. The series of quests on this floor were titled the "Ruby Key," which meant the trial would not be over until we had acquired it.

Once she let go, I asked her something I'd always wondered.

"Listen…On the sixth floor, you said that only the knight commander or the queen herself could rebuke you. So why were you being held prisoner in Harin Tree Palace?"

"Oh…that?" Kizmel said, her expression tightening. She huffed and said, "It might trivialize it to say that my timing was poor… You see, there is a high priest staying in Harin at the moment. He has the same level of authority as a knight commander."

"Um…That *is* unlucky…" I said, doing my best not to wallow in the moment. I stifled the feeling and went on, "But if we get the sacred key from this floor and deliver it to Harin Tree Palace, the suspicions placed on you will be cleared up, won't they?"

However, the knight just looked away and shook her head.

"Unfortunately, it is not that simple. Because of the suspicion I am under, the Pagoda Knights Brigade itself has been removed from the duty of recovering the keys. Tomorrow a retrieval team will be sent from either the Sandalwood or Trifoliate Knights by the royal palace. They will head for the shrine of the sacred key on this floor. If I retrieve the key before them, or if we encounter one another at the shrine, it will only complicate the problem."

"Mmmmm..."

It sounded plenty complex already. I tried my best to organize the facts around the campaign quest as I understood them.

The entire reason the dark elves were recovering the six sacred keys from their shrines scattered across the third floor to the eighth was because they had received intelligence that the enemy forest elves were attempting to do the same.

The three knight brigades squabbled over who would have the honor of the duty, and in the end, it was the Pagoda Knights, known for their light and nimble gear, who were chosen to recover the keys. The advance team of a few dozen dispatched to the third floor included Kizmel and her herbalist sister, Tilnel.

That group encountered a forest elf unit in the woods and did battle. Many lost their lives, including Tilnel. The advance team's commander, attempting to continue the mission with half of their number, split them into multiple squads to distract the forest elves and send a single member to retrieve the key. It was Kizmel who volunteered for that dangerous duty.

Kizmel succeeded at recovering the Jade Key from the third-floor shrine, but on the way back to camp, she encountered a forest elf knight and fought him. It was nearly a mutual defeat when Asuna and I entered the fray, and we succeeded in defeating the forest elf knight, which I wasn't able to do in the beta.

After that, the two of us officially became Kizmel's partners on her quest, helping her gain the sacred keys on the fourth, fifth, and sixth floors. But when the members of Qusack, a small guild we met at Castle Galey, were taken hostage by the man in the black poncho from the PK gang, he'd demanded Kizmel leave the castle with the four keys. When we'd arrived, the Fallen Elf adjutant Kysarah had appeared, overwhelmed us with great force, and stole all the sacred keys.

The timing couldn't have been a coincidence. We also had corroborating evidence: Morte and the dagger user from the same gang had a Fallen Elf dagger and poisoned throwing picks. That suggested that, somehow, two of the biggest threats in Aincrad, the PK gang and the Fallen Elves, were working together. But the more pressing problem now was the internal strife among the dark elves.

If angering the priests who were in charge of the key-retrieval project caused Kizmel's Pagoda Knights to be removed from the mission, then it was our fault, for begging her to take the keys out of the castle. Yes, it was to save Qusack from a terrible fate, but that was a human—a player—problem, and the dark elves weren't obligated to intercede on our behalf. But Kizmel had taken the keys out of the castle without a second thought. We had no choice but to help dispel the stain we'd put on her reputation.

"…Mmmm."

Moments later, having composed my thoughts, I looked up.

"Meaning that if the Sandalwood or Trifoliate Knights fail at their retrieval mission, there's no problem with us sweeping in after and picking up the key?"

Kizmel and Asuna made expressions of skepticism that were so similar they looked like sisters.

"Kirito, you're not suggesting that we interfere with the retrieval team, are you?"

"That's right, Kirito. That would be crossing a line, and you know it."

"I-I'm not! I'm not!" I protested hastily, trying to come up with a proper explanation.

The reason I mentioned the new retrieval team failing was because this was *Asuna's and my quest*. RPG quests were designed by their nature to test the player. Naturally, it would be the easiest quest in the world if some NPCs were going to come along and complete the task for us.

On the other hand, there was such a thing as timed competitive quests. You competed with NPCs on a certain task. If you beat them, you completed the quest, and if you failed, it was over. If the "Ruby Key" quest turned out like one of them, it was possible that we could fail the "Elf War" questline at the moment a different retrieval team got the key, and that would be the end of our involvement.

But I could not explain that logic to Kizmel. This wasn't a game or a quest to her. It was her actual duty and her actual life.

If I opened my window and checked the quest log now, the updated quest text might point out the correct direction to go. But I did not want to do that in front of her for the same reason. We ought to think for ourselves and make the decision that seemed best to us.

"...Kizmel, where's the shrine for the sacred key on this floor, again?" I asked, considering the possibility that it had been moved since the beta. The knight put a hand to her chin to think, then pointed toward the labyrinth tower.

"I cannot be certain because I have not seen the official orders, but I believe it was somewhat south of the Pillar of the Heavens."

Then it hadn't changed. It would be less than an hour west of Pramio, a town between Volupta and the labyrinth tower.

"Okay...and the new retrieval team is coming to the seventh floor tomorrow? Can you guess what time of day that might be...?" I asked, knowing it was impossible to answer.

Kizmel just grimaced and said, "I could not tell you the hour. But the messenger must head to the spirit tree north of Harin Tree Palace and travel to the castle on the ninth floor, then the priests must give the mission to either the Sandalwood Knights or the Trifoliate Knights, allowing them time to assemble a retrieval team and go back down the spirit tree to the seventh floor. All of that will be impossible by the end of today. If they leave the ninth floor on the morn, traveling from the spirit tree to the sacred key shrine will last them until at least midday, at the earliest."

"Midday..." I repeated. Based on that, I decided to make a decision and let the chips fall where they may. I inhaled, exhaled, then gave Kizmel and Asuna a look. "Because we cannot recover the Ruby Key ourselves, the only way to restore Kizmel's honor is to recover the four lost keys instead."

"Huh...?" Asuna blurted out.

"What?" Kizmel demanded.

"Are you sure about this, Kirito? I mean, if we can do that, it would be the quickest way...but we don't even know where the keys are now!" Asuna said rapidly.

I looked at Kizmel again and said, "I suspect that the Fallen Elves are going to attack the Ruby Key retrieval team after they leave the shrine. That's how it's almost always gone anyway."

"......"

Kizmel said nothing. I knew that the plan I was about to detail would bump right up against her personal line between good and evil.

"We're going to hide near the exit of the shrine, then follow the retrieval team when they emerge with the key. If the Fallen Elves attack, we'll watch for a little bit. If the retrieval team beats them without a problem, we'll follow the retreating Fallen. If they look like they're going to lose, we'll join the fight to help, then chase the fleeing Fallen back to their hideout."

Kizmel did not say anything for quite a while after I was done. Five seconds later, she murmured, "So you want to use the retrieval team as a decoy."

"Uh...n-no, I'm saying that the Fallen are probably going to attack whether we're there or not, so it's not like the team is a decoy. Plus, if they're in danger, we'll be helping out in the battle...So if you want to view it fairly, it's like eighty percent helping others and twenty percent using them. In my opinion."

"......"

Kizmel was silent again. I was starting to think my attempt to convince her was a failure, when the knight's shoulders trembled, and she finally burst into chuckles.

"Ha—ha-ha-ha...Oh, Kirito, there you go again. When Sir Lavik said that humanity has a power uniquely its own, perhaps he was referring to your utter boldness."

I couldn't even protest with *Really? You'd say that about this sweet, naïve youth?* before Asuna laughed. "Ah-ha-ha-ha, he's right about that. Even I couldn't have come up with a plan like that."

I wasn't so sure about *that*, but I'd been partners with Asuna for long enough to know not to say so out loud. I kept it to myself, clearing my throat rather loudly, then asked the two women, "So are we agreed on this direction?"

"Well, I suppose it works." "I agree."

With Kizmel and Asuna on board, I glanced at the clock readout. It was still barely after eight o'clock in the morning. We'd come out of the west end of Looserock Forest rather than the south, so the trip was a little longer, but we could get back to Volupta by ten without hurrying. That would easily put us well ahead of the one o'clock deadline from Nirrnir. But perhaps it would be better to move quickly and help out Argo with her lonely task of collecting wurtz stones.

That was assuming Kizmel agreed to the detour to Volupta, however. Of course, she had seemed curious of Stachion on the sixth floor, so she probably wouldn't protest, I assumed.

I turned to her and started off by saying, "So, Kizmel, there's something else I want to ask you about..."

12

ARGO HAD ONLY BRIEFLY MET KIZMEL BEFORE THE fourth-floor boss fight, so it was more or less her first real encounter with the dark elf. But after interacting with other high-functioning AI NPCs like Myia, Theano, Nirrnir, and Kio, she welcomed the guest and took her presence in stride.

Even still, the Rat was surprised that Kizmel, a companion NPC from the "Elf War" campaign quest, agreed to help with the totally unrelated task of gathering wurtz stones. She kept looking over at Asuna and the dark elf knight, who were chatting happily as we searched for stones in the wide riverbed, and murmured things to herself like "Hmm" and "Well, well." I wanted to believe that it wasn't because she was getting some wicked ideas—like using Kizmel as a tool to gain more experience points.

As for the wurtz stones, they were little black rocks less than an inch in size. While they had a particular metallic shine to them, I had to agree that it would be extremely inefficient to try to search for them in the middle of the night. On top of that, there were faux wurtz pieces that looked the same except for the lack of that shine, plus river crabs that appeared identical in color and texture until they snipped at your fingers with their claws, just to make things that much more annoying.

Regardless, Argo had already found over twenty, so with the four of us together, it took less than an hour to reach the necessary total. Once our quest log had updated properly, Argo took out some bottled fruit juice from her inventory to celebrate, and we headed directly east into Volupta.

As she did when going into Stachion on the floor below, Kizmel wore a dark hooded cloak that hid her face and her armor. I was a bit nervous when we passed through the gate, but the NPC guards showed no sign of suspicion when we went through.

The west gate of Volupta was actually on the northwest corner of the city, because it had been built along the waterline. The white buildings and blue roofs were visible the instant you walked through the gate. Kizmel came to a stop in the small open space and simply observed for a moment.

"This is...a beautiful place," she murmured. "Stachion had too many squares for my liking, but I would enjoy staying in this town for a time, I think. Is that the sea to the south?"

I wasn't quite sure how to answer that. "Well, since it's part of Aincrad, I don't think you can call it a sea, exactly...but it is saltwater."

"Then, most likely, this land was carved off the coastline when the Great Separation occurred," she said.

"Oh," exclaimed Asuna. "Of course, that's right. Then maybe there's a floor that's just, like, one little island, which would leave the majority of it as sea."

Logically speaking, that was sound. I was impressed by Asuna's power of imagination. "That would make beating it really easy. I mean, once you leave the main town, the labyrinth tower's got to be right in front of you, huh?"

Asuna and Kizmel both sighed with exasperation, and Argo just shook her head. I cleared my throat awkwardly and tried to save face by changing the topic.

"Um, oh yeah! If we get our hands on a pass, we should take Kizmel to the beach, too. You've never been in the ocean, have you?"

"No, of course not...But what do you mean by a pass?" the knight asked suspiciously. I explained the limited access system that applied to the entire beach, but it did not answer her question. "I am surprised the townspeople agreed to such a rule," she said. "Who is forbidding them from going there?"

"Umm...the person we're about to meet...I guess..."

As soon as the words were out of my mouth, I regretted it. Kizmel was a proud dark elf knight. Nirrnir was a refined lady with even more pride than the elf. And Kio was a battle maid with absolute loyalty to her master. There was no way they'd all get along. It was a bad idea making Nirrnir look worse before they even had a chance to meet...but we couldn't just leave Kizmel on her own outside the casino.

Praying that we'd never have to see either Kizmel or Kio— or both—draw their weapons in polite company, I said, "Well, um...shall we get going?"

It wasn't even noon yet, but the Volupta Grand Casino had guests streaming in and out of the building. Fortunately, I didn't see any ALS or DKB members. Asuna sent Liten a message to ask about them, and she replied that they held a late-night drinking session under the guise of a "meeting for reflection" after their massive loss at the arena. Both guilds were likely to resume activities after noon.

Of course, they only lost big in the sense that their fifty thousand chips (five million col) had all come from winning by following the cheat sheet—the actual loss from their assets was the original eleven thousand col they'd converted to chips. Of course, even that wasn't chump change, and if it had happened to me, I'd be there drinking, too.

Were Lind and Kibaou planning on trying out the monster battle again today? Or were they going to forget about the totally broken Sword of Volupta and focus on beating the floor instead?

I was hoping it was the latter—not because I was judging them, but because I knew that there was cheating and conspiracy afoot in the arena. The Korloys were probably cheating in some way in a majority of the ten matches throughout the day, bilking their guests out of extra chips. The man who sold the ALS and DKB that cheat sheet had to be an agent of the Korloy family, too.

Then again, that man was at the west gate of Lectio, the first town of the floor. To get the cheat sheets for today, you'd have to walk all the way to Lectio and back. Lind and Kibaou weren't going to do that, and I doubted they would jump into the arena without that betting information on hand. As I'd told Asuna this morning, I suspected the two were viewing that eleven thousand col as an expensive lesson learned. Or at least, I hoped they did.

We went into the Grand Casino. Argo showed off her pass and got us up to the third floor, where we walked down the dimly lit hallway of the luxury hotel and came to a stop in front of Room 17.

Like yesterday, Argo knocked on the door twice. From inside, Kio asked, "Who is it?"

"It's Argo. Also, my companions…er, my three assistants."

"You found another one?"

"Don't worry, this one's much more capable than Kirito."

I briefly took offense to that before conceding that it was definitely true. The lock clicked, and the door swung open.

Argo went in first, followed by Asuna, Kizmel, then me. I checked the time—it was eleven thirty. We were ninety minutes ahead of the one o'clock deadline Nirrnir gave us. That didn't mean she was going to pay us a bonus, and it was Argo who took the quest anyway. Asuna and I weren't getting money, just the knowledge of how to find Snow Tree Buds.

The spacious suite was just as dark as last night, despite the midday hour. The windows were completely blocked with thick curtains, and only a few humble lamps—not bonfire shrooms—lit the room.

The large sofa in the middle of the chamber was empty. I blinked with surprise, and Kio addressed us with some contrition.

"Lady Nirrnir is still asleep. She will be awake by noon. Will you have some tea and wait until then?"

"Well, of course. It's our fault for comin' early," said Argo. Kio's eyes traveled past her and onto us—specifically, Kizmel, with her hood pulled low. The woman's sharp eyes narrowed.

"Is that another adventurer?"

"...No..."

Kizmel hesitated, then slowly pulled back her hood. The reaction was instantaneous.

"Lyusulian!" Kio cried, placing a hand on her estoc. Kizmel did not grab the hilt of her saber but did pull her left foot back into a sideways stance.

I took a quick step forward and asked, "What's Lyusulian?" Asuna whispered, "I think it's a person from Lyusula." Seeing the logic in it, I promptly asked Kio, "What do you call a person from Kales'Oh?"

The battle maid, despite her stern expression, replied, "A Kalessian."

"Ohhh."

"But why is there a Lyusulian here?!"

"Why? Uh, because she's with us..."

Amid the uproar, the door on the left wall opened, and a small figure came into the living room, slippers slapping against the floor.

"What is all this noise about...?"

It was a yawning girl, with buoyant golden hair down past her waist, blindingly white skin, and brilliant eyes as red as gemstones. She held a large pillow with her left arm and wore a black nightgown. Above her head was a three-dimensional *?* icon, the sign of a quest in progress.

Nirrnir, head of the Nachtoys, one of the two families who controlled the Volupta Grand Casino, stopped in front of the empty five-person sofa and faced us. She was the shortest of anyone here, but it felt like she was gazing down at us from on high.

Kio had been an instant away from drawing her estoc, but now she bowed in shame for the disturbance. She did not move away from her confrontational position with Kizmel, however.

And as for Kizmel, what she did left my mouth hanging open with shock.

I assumed she would merely watch Nirrnir in silence, but instead, she knelt on the carpet with one knee. She pressed her right hand to her chest and lowered her head deeply.

"I am Kizmel, knight of Lyusula. Please forgive me for disturbing your rest."

Out of the corner of my eye, I could see Asuna gape in surprise.

Nirrnir did have a certain air to her that was unlike any little girl I'd ever met, and she was the descendant of Falhari, the hero who founded Volupta, but at most, she was a casino boss, not a noble or royalty. Yet the proud knight knelt to her in a show of great deference. She hadn't even done that for Viscount Yofilis.

Nirrnir, however, just nodded as though this were perfectly ordinary.

"Don't worry, Kizmel. You were helping Argo's group, weren't you? Then you are my guest as well. Please raise your head and have a seat. Bring tea, Kio."

"…Shouldn't I take her sword, my lady?" asked Kio.

The young master stifled a yawn and answered, "No, you needn't bother. A knight of Lyusula wouldn't undertake an assassination."

She dropped the pillow she was cradling onto the center of the five-seat sofa, which already had plenty of cushions, and sat down right next to it.

Kizmel stood up again, so we moved over to the couches. Argo and I sat on the three-person sofa across from her, while Kizmel and Asuna sat on the big one. Kio brought out cups for the table and poured us freshly made tea. I thanked her and took a sip.

This was a different tea from yesterday's and smelled like citrus rather than grape, but it was just as tasty. But while it tasted good, what I really wanted was something to eat with it. From the early morning until now, the only thing I'd had was a nibble of extremely shocking narsos fruit. But I couldn't order a meal here, of course, and Asuna looked perfectly fine despite having eaten no more than me. So I tensed my gut and held my hunger in.

This time, Nirrnir had tea instead of wine, probably because it was the middle of the day. After a short while, she had awakened enough to look at Argo and ask, "So…did you gather what I asked of you?"

"Of course. Should I take 'em out now?"

"Not just yet. Kio, two large bowls."

"Right away."

Kio went to a cabinet against the wall and took out two large silver bowls, which she placed on the table. Nirrnir held out a palm toward them.

Argo and I shared a look, then opened our inventories. I materialized a large cloth sack, and Argo produced a small one, which we emptied into the bowls.

Nirrnir first picked up one of the poisonous-looking narsos fruits, staring at it closely before putting it back. Next she plucked up a wurtz stone, examined it, and dropped it in the bowl.

"…Twenty ripe narsos fruits and fifty wurtz stones, just as I asked. Well done…Kio, the payment."

The maid took out a small leather sack and handed it to Argo, who said "A pleasure doin' business!" right as the *?* mark over Nirrnir's head vanished.

But a split second later, another *!* appeared. The quest continued after this. Nirrnir took a sip of tea, then said, mostly to herself, "This will make the bleaching agent I need. The Rusty Lykaon will appear in the second match of the night, so there's plenty of time. The problem is…I suspect the Korloys may be wary that their fur-dyeing scheme has been discovered."

"Even if they are, can they withdraw a monster that has already been registered for the competition?" asked not me, nor Asuna, nor Argo—but none other than Kizmel.

We'd given her a basic rundown of the situation on the way to the casino, but this was truly a remarkable level of understanding.

I didn't want to believe it was just because she was an AI with all the answers available to her. Kizmel—and all the high-functioning NPCs in *SAO*—thought for herself, questioned, wondered, and sometimes made mistakes in the search of the best possible solution to any question.

And Nirrnir, who probably had an AI just as advanced as Kizmel's, nodded and said, "That is correct. A beast once registered *must* appear in combat. In the long history of the Grand Casino, that rule has only been broken twice...Once was when a Korloy family servant forgot to give the creature its food, and their hold on the beast was broken before the match, requiring it to be exterminated. The other time was when a Nachtoy child snuck into the stables behind the casino and felt sorry for the creature, allowing it to escape. Both were very foolish mistakes."

There was undeniable scorn in her voice. Kio looked like she wanted to say something, but recovered and returned to her usual stoic look.

Kizmel continued, "Then whether the Korloy family is wary or not, the plan to bleach the dye out of the lykaon's fur—I did not know narsos fruit could be used to do such a thing—should not be affected in any way."

"It will not...I believe. But I would rather be thorough." Nirrnir looked at the girl next to me. "Argo, I doubt the Korloys are aware of you yet. Would you be willing to apply the bleach to the lykaon's fur as well?"

"Mm, mmm..."

Argo's noncommittal answer was probably because she was thinking of Asuna, Kizmel, and me, and we had a very important mission of our own to worry about. But according to Kizmel's expectations, the dark elf key retrieval team would not arrive until midday tomorrow, and as a gambler who once bet everything at this monster arena, I wanted to find out the conclusion of this conspiracy.

I gave her a look that said *We're fine*, so Argo nodded and turned to Nirrnir again.

"Sure thing. We'll do it."

"I am glad to hear it," Nirrnir said, smiling, as the icon over her head turned into a question mark. She swallowed the rest of her tea, then clapped her hands. "In that case, we must mix that bleaching solution. Kio, prepare a pot."

"Uh…we're doing it here?" I asked with surprise, which earned me a withering look from the maid.

"Did you think we were going to make it in the casino kitchen? Where the Korloys would know about it within five seconds?"

"Oh…yeah. Good point. Of course."

"As punishment for your foolish question, you are called upon to help, Kirito."

There wasn't a new quest log message, so that meant it wasn't an official quest, just a task. But at this point, I had no good reason to refuse.

"I-I'd be happy to."

"Then you may start by squeezing the juice from the narsos fruit."

"Okay…but with what tool?"

"You have perfectly fine tools on the end of your arms."

Apparently, I was supposed to squeeze them by hand. I wasn't sure if that was really what they wanted, but I'd never seen any juicers or mixers in Aincrad.

"The juice will go in here," said Kio, presenting me with a glass bowl. I picked up one of the narsos out of the silver bowl. Based on its pear-like texture, I suspected that if I squeezed it with all my strength, it would burst into chunks. So I held it over the glass bowl, adding pressure to my fingers bit by bit, until the light green lines running across the purplish-red skin split, forcefully expelling a milky white juice over my fingers and into the bowl.

A moment later, the spicy-sweet scent wafted up, and I was remembering how nice the flavor was, if not for the nasty electric-shock sensation…

Zzzap! My palms stung as though hit by supercharged static electricity, and I screamed and tossed the squeezed fruit.

"Aaaaah!!"

As I writhed, holding my right hand in the air, Nirrnir flopped over onto her side and cackled with laughter.

"Ah-ha-ha! Ah-ha-ha-ha-ha-ha!!"

"Aauugh…Y-you knew about this, Miss Nirr!"

"Ah-ha-ha-ha-ha-ha! The way you went *Aaaaah!!* Ah-ha-ha-ha-ha-ha!!"

She kicked her legs uproariously and rolled back and forth. I wanted to jump onto her and tickle her until she cried, but I knew it wouldn't be appropriate behavior toward a young lady in her nightgown, plus it would probably earn me some puncture wounds from Kio's estoc.

As I withstood the remnants of the shocking sensation, I saw that Argo, Asuna, and Kizmel were also laughing. With a moment of horror, I looked up and saw that even Kio had her back turned to me and was trembling.

It's fine, I told myself. *As long as everyone has a nice little moment of entertainment to blow off stress.*

Then I realized that there were still nineteen narsos fruits left to squeeze, and I exhaled heavily through my nose.

13

ONE HOUR LATER, AT 12:50 PM, I WAS WANDERING around the game room on the first floor of the Grand Casino.

Nirrnir gave me waterproof leather gloves for squeezing the fruit, so I didn't have to suffer the nasty shock twice. I told her vengefully that she could have given them to me from the start, and all she said was, "But that wouldn't have been funny."

Kio transferred the bowlful of juice to a thick copper pot, then sank the fifty wurtz stones into it and started the fire. If it was simmered on a low heat for three hours, it should make a small vial of the decolorant bleach. It made me wonder why we didn't get twice the materials for a backup vial, but I supposed it was one of those RPG situations where you were meant to have just one chance to make it count. But all we had to do was stand at the front closest to the cage, then spray the lykaon with the solution before the fight. It was nearly impossible to fail, it seemed to me.

Nirrnir left Kio in charge of the flames and took Asuna, Argo, and Kizmel to the hotel's spa—I was invited, too, but respectfully declined. I got a pass for the stairs and went down to the first floor, headed for the bar counter in the playroom, and ordered a club sandwich to fill my stomach. Satisfied at last, I decided to wander around the room for a bit.

That was when I noticed a large player watching a roulette table. He wore a loud shirt over khaki shorts and had long blond hair pulled back with a thin hairband. It was the two-handed-sword user from the DKB, Hafner the "soccer player." I didn't see any of his guildmates around.

I was going to give him a wide berth and avoid notice, except that something stuck out to me. According to Liten, the DKB was going to resume activity at noon. But here was one of their primary members, Hafner, wandering around the casino all alone.

After thinking it over, I snuck up behind him and slapped him on the back. "How ya doin', Haf?"

He twitched and turned around, then made a sour face when he recognized me.

"...Hey, Black. Don't call me by that nickname. We're not friends."

"You just called me a nickname."

"Well...okay, whatever," he snorted, then looked around. "Your partner's not with you?"

I wisely chose not to mention that she was in the bath right now. "Not at the moment. What about you, Haf? I heard the DKB was hitting the road again at noon."

"Yeah...most of the members are out there crushing quests and leveling up," he admitted. I supposed he was just honest by nature. But I wasn't, so I used that leverage against him.

"Then what are you doing here? Shouldn't one of the sub-leaders be out there watching over the newbies?"

"I don't have a choice. I've got a different job to do."

"Job...? This?" I pointed to the roulette table.

The man winced. "No, not gambling. Supposedly, if I hang out here before the monster battles start, the guy who sells the cheat sheets is gonna come by..."

He suddenly clamped his mouth shut so hard, his teeth clicked. He grimaced.

"Crap! I didn't need to mention that. Just get outta here, man."

But after hearing that, there was no way I could back down. There were some rather ominous key words in that little admission.

"H-hang on. Are you talking about the guy who spoke to you at the gate in Lectio yesterday?"

"Now how would you know about something like that, Black?"

"Just answer the question. The sheet seller from Lectio is going to show up here? Who told you that?" I pressed him.

Hafner's expression got even uglier, but he answered the question anyway. "I don't know who. Someone in the guild heard the rumor. It might not be true anyway. See, look over there."

I glanced in the direction he was surreptitiously pointing. There was a familiar player staked out at a distant roulette table. It was…the trident user from the ALS, Hokkai Ikura.

"Couple more ALS folks playing poker and craps, too. I bet they're all after the cheat sheet guy."

"…Meaning the DKB and ALS are both intent on the monster battle today, too…?" I asked, aghast.

Hafner glared at me. "Maybe you're wondering why we haven't learned our lesson yet. Well, you saw the ridiculous specs on that sword, right?" He pointed his thumb behind him at the exchange counter in the center of the room—and the golden longsword that outshone everything else at the top of the prize area. "If you get that sword, you'd be unstoppable not just on this floor, but through at least the tenth. You're a one-handed sword guy, too. Don't tell me you wouldn't want it."

"I'm not going to deny it…The thing is, Kibaou's a one-handed sword user, but your Lind uses a scimitar, doesn't he? What's he going to do, change his main weapon skill?"

"No way, Lind's not that big of a skinflint. It'll probably end up going to Shivata if we get the sword."

Shivata was another sub-leader of the DKB, the track-and-field-looking guy—and he did use a one-handed sword. That made sense to me.

"…But in the arena yesterday, you bet on the favorite according to the cheat sheet every time and lost everything at the end, didn't you? How do you know the same thing won't happen today?"

"Seriously, how do you know all that…?" Hafner wondered,

scowling again. He folded his arms, a clear signal that he was done talking. "Everything past this point is a company secret. Now get lost, for real this time. I've got to catch myself a sheet seller."

Yeah, and that guy's almost guaranteed to be a Korloy cat's-paw.

But I couldn't tell him that. Hafner wouldn't believe me at this point. He probably hadn't even heard the name Korloy yet.

"Fine, fine," I said. "Thanks for the info, though. I'll let you in on a little tip."

"...What?"

"See how the roulette dealer's wearing a bow tie with a black-and-red pattern? If there's more black than red on the tie, the ball's more likely to land black. Same thing's true of red."

"...Seriously?" Hafner's eyes went wide.

I smirked. "It's only about a sixty-forty split, though. Can't take it too literally. See ya."

With a wave, I left the roulette table, and the smile left my face.

Something was fishy if the DKB and ALS were embarking on another big gambling run, relying on the cheat sheets. And this time, the seller wasn't approaching them directly but was supposedly using a more elaborate ruse, by showing up if they sat around gambling. The difference made it seem much less that they were being ripped off by a scammer.

If the result of the gamble was that someone ended up with the Sword of Volupta legitimately, that was a good thing, but I doubted it would happen. The Korloys had to be plotting a variety of tricks again to take advantage of the two guilds.

I returned to the main hall from the gaming room and headed for the stairs, intent on discussing this with the rest of the group. But I stopped when I realized they might not be back from the spa yet. If I wanted to maximize the use of this time, I could still collect a bit more information.

In fact, Nirrnir had said something earlier that caught my interest—a story about a child who'd snuck into the stable behind the casino and let one of the monsters free out of an abundance of pity, or something...

During the beta test, I thought I had searched every nook and cranny of the casino that was accessible, but I did not know there was a stable behind the back of the building. If there were twenty monsters fighting in the Battle Arena per day, there had to be a place for them to wait. Maybe I'd learn something if I went to check it out.

I passed many visitors in the main hallway and left the casino, then came to a stop in front of the deluxe facade and pretended to be indecisive about which way to go, using the opportunity to examine the area.

If you walked down the stairs from the marble porch of the building, the front gate was just ahead, but there were smaller staircases to the right and left, with small paths running through the decorative plants. I worried about the guards standing on either side of the entrance, but if you weren't allowed to go in those directions, they would have closed them off to start with, I figured. So I casually stepped down the stairs and headed down the left path.

After twenty meters of carefully manicured plants, the path came to an abrupt dead end. A black wrought iron gate blocked the way, about eight feet tall.

The path on the other side of the building was probably the same way. I'd have to get over this gate to reach the back side of the casino. Somewhere on the rear side of the lot was most likely a gate for ushering in the tamed monsters, and it stood to reason that it was more tightly guarded than the front entrance.

At my current strength and agility, it would be impossible to get over an eight-foot gate with a vertical jump. I probably wouldn't be able to achieve a feat like that until I was level 80 or 90. Hopefully this game of death was beaten before then, but until then, I put myself to the task of checking the sides of the gate.

The right half of the gate was fixed to the wall that surrounded the casino grounds, and there was nothing on its surface that offered purchase for climbing. But the left gate was attached to the wall of the building, which had alternating marble blocks that stuck out about an inch. It was just barely usable as a handhold— the real question was if I'd be branded a criminal for crossing this fence. Then again, if I did, there ought to be a warning message, like with thievery and inappropriate contact.

If the message appears, I'll get out at once, I told myself, looking over my shoulder. There were no other visitors or guards on the tiled path. I stepped up to the wall and placed a hand on one of the blocks that jutted out.

I couldn't get more than my first finger joint for leverage, but the challenge of the climb was far lower than the outer wall mountain of Castle Galey on the previous floor. For one thing, I was so close to the ground I couldn't possibly suffer any damage in a fall. I steadied my breathing, then used the fingertips of both hands and my toes to grab the wall, and climbed. Once I was above the height of the fence, I moved horizontally to the right. After I was sure the ground below was clear, I jumped off.

My knees absorbed the impact upon landing. I waited in my landing crouch for several seconds, but no guards came rushing over to get me. No warning messages, either.

I stood up and looked around the area. The narrow path and decorative plants were the same as on the other side, but they felt slightly less manicured over here.

Sneaking forward down the path, I soon came to a left turn. I hugged the corner of the building and peered around. Once again, there was nothing but a path running between the building and the wall that surrounded it.

If I kept going, it should take me around the rear of the casino. But the path here was probably a good hundred meters long, and if any guards came around the corner in either direction, there was nowhere to escape. If they caught me, I'd be banned from the casino at best, or imprisoned, or turned into an orange player at worst.

Was it worth taking that much of a risk to investigate this possible stable?

I considered it for a moment, then began walking forward, not back.

If Nirrnir's strategy to bleach the dye out of the lykaon's fur worked, the Korloys' scheme would be brought into the sunlight—or into the underground hall at night, at least—and she'd have the chance to punish the mysterious Bardun Korloy for his crime. Maybe we'd even get back the twenty thousand-plus col they cheated the ALS and DKB out of yesterday.

But that didn't eliminate the possibility that the Korloy family had another trick up their sleeve. If the plan failed for some reason, and both guilds suffered even greater losses than before, not only could it come with major monetary damage, but it could also severely damage Lind's and Kibaou's drive to succeed. The loss of all my wealth in the beta was a funny story now, but if the foundation beneath the feet of the game's best players in the official release became unstable, that could have a profound effect on many people's lives. With the specter of the PK gang and Fallen Elves looming overhead, the last thing we needed was another major source of trouble.

Suddenly, I felt an icy sensation on my back, and I stood still.

I turned back, but there was no one behind me. The cause of the chill was my own train of thought.

Was it possible they were behind *this*, too? After the fifth and sixth floors, was the PK gang plotting to trip up the ALS and DKB from a new, unexpected angle?

No, I was just being paranoid. We passed through the seventh-floor teleport gate at midnight on January 5. The DKB and ALS reached Volupta that same morning. There just couldn't have been any time for the PK gang to make contact with the Korloys and propose a scam, and it just didn't seem possible in the first place. The whole reason we were helping Nirrnir in the first place was because Argo had undertaken her quest.

I was overthinking things. If the man in the black poncho and his followers could agitate not just players but NPCs, too, then they were true—...

I stopped that thought in its tracks and headed down the shaded pathway, deeper into darkness.

(To be continued)

AFTERWORD

Thank you for reading *Sword Art Online Progressive 7*, "Rhapsody of Crimson Heat (Part One)."

First of all, I want to apologize that just after doing it with the sixth floor, I am again writing a two-book story. When I started, I thought casually to myself, *I'll only write about the casino and the beach, and it'll be done before I know it*, but then we didn't get to the casino for a while, and there's conspiracy afoot when we get there, and we can't ignore the stolen keys from the sixth floor—so the story grew more and more in the telling, until I finally realized I had to write my editor and say, "I'm sorry, it has to be a two-parter..."

I think the biggest reason the story ballooned so much is that it's just really fun for me to write scenes where Kirito and Asuna are traveling alone, fighting monsters, and eating food and such. In the *Unital Ring* arc, which I'm writing in parallel with this, there are tons of other friends around, plus Kirito's the leader of the attack team, while Asuna's the leader of the defense team, which separates their duties, meaning there are almost no scenes with just the two of them. So as a reaction to that, I ended up writing lots of those scenes in this book...but I feel like that's also a big draw of the *Progressive* series, so I hope you all enjoyed them, too.

The story was just getting into the depths of the conspiracy around the casino when I hit you with that "to be continued," but the next volume that finishes this floor should be out soon, if my schedule works out. I want to make sure you're not waiting too long, so I hope you can hold out. In the next volume, we should see plenty of Kizmel, of course, as well as Argo and the other players, plus the mysterious Nirrnir and her battle maid, Kio, whom you'll notice did not actually do any battling yet. Look forward to it!

And speaking of *Progressive*! As of January 2021, when I'm writing this afterword, the theatrical movie *Sword Art Online Progressive: Aria of a Starless Night* is in full-powered production. The book should be coming out in Japan right around the time they announce a date for its release, I think. It retells the story of the first floor with extra focus on Asuna, so if you've read the first volume of *SAOP* or watched the first season of the anime, I hope the movie will give you a new perspective on the story. Look forward to it, folks!

Lastly, to my illustrator, abec, whom I dragged into my tough schedule right at the start of the year, and my editors, Miki and Adachi, I'm so sorry once again! It'll be another tough year, I'm sure, but let's all get through it as a team along with our readers!

Reki Kawahara—January 2021

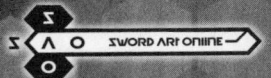

What awaits our hero in the darkness lurking behind the casino...?

And then—a great and terrible change comes over Kirito...Don't miss the thrilling eighth volume, coming soon!

SWORD ART ONLINE PROGRESSIVE

VOLUME 8
COMING SOON!